D1330872

BROOK EVANS

Persephone Book N°26
Published by Persephone Books Ltd 2001

Reprinted 2009

First published in 1928
by Victor Gollancz in the UK and
Frederick Stokes in the US
© The Estate of Susan Glaspell

Endpapers taken from a block-printed linen designed and
manufactured in New York by Pierre Chareau in 1928,
reproduced by courtesy of the Trustees of the
Victoria & Albert Museum, London

Typeset in ITC Baskerville by Keystroke,
Jacaranda Lodge, Wolverhampton

Printed by the MPG Books Group in the UK

ISBN 978 1 903155 165

Persephone Books Ltd
59 Lamb's Conduit Street
London WC1N 3NB

www.persephonebooks.co.uk

BROOK EVANS

by

SUSAN GLASPELL

PERSEPHONE BOOKS
LONDON

PUBLISHER'S NOTE

༄༅༅༅༅༅

Brook Evans was the very first book to be published with the distinctive Gollancz yellow cover; Victor Gollancz (who was to be a great supporter of women writers) chose – indeed begged Susan Glaspell for permission – to launch the first list of his new firm with her novel in the spring of 1928.

It was her fourth book, published thirteen years after *Fidelity* (1915), Persephone Book No. 4. Before she wrote *Fidelity* Susan Glaspell had lived at home, attended the University of Iowa, been a journalist, and written two popular and successful novels. Then, in the years after 1915, she and her husband George Cram 'Jig' Cook became the centre of a group of experimental playwrights that included Eugene O'Neill; later they moved to Greece. At this period she wrote mainly plays and short stories, and it was only after her husband's death in 1924 and her new life with a younger lover that she returned to prose fiction, *Brook Evans* being her first book at this time.

A novel about love, it is constructed like a play or symphony in three acts or movements, the first set in 1888, the second in 1907 and the third (and the coda) in 1928. Thematically it is similar to *Fidelity*, in that it is about a young girl wanting to be true to herself and her love but thereby finding herself at odds with social convention; again it asks the question – should she put love first? But this time Susan Glaspell gives a slightly different answer.

She was familiar with the *avant-garde* thinking of her time and was deeply interested in Nietzsche's ideas about the need for a radical change in moral values – ideas also adopted by D.H.Lawrence, whose *Lady Chatterley's Lover* was written at the same time as *Brook Evans* and published in the same month.

The reviews of Susan Glaspell's book were mostly ecstatic: the *Glasgow Herald* wrote, 'We have no hesitation in saying that this novel is one of the few works of genius that have come from America'; the *Observer* commented: 'The beginning almost takes one's breath away with its simple courage . . . There is enough beauty in the first fifty pages to make the whole live in memory and gratitude'; and the writer Storm Jameson observed that *Brook Evans* 'is actually what its publishers say it is: a profound, frank and beautiful love story.'

Brook Evans was filmed by Paramount as *The Right to Love* in 1931, the same year that Susan Glaspell won the Pulitzer Prize for her play, *Alison's House*.

For more information about her work the reader is referred to the Persephone Preface to *Fidelity*.

∿∿∿∿∿∿∿

BROOK EVANS

BOOK ONE

CHAPTER I

HER mother came into the kitchen, looked at the peas which did not yet cover the bottom of the yellow dish, at the basket still heaped with peas in pod, laughed indulgently: "Naomi!" When indulgent the *o* in her daughter's name was round and long. "What in the world you thinking about?"

Naomi smiled as she pressed a pod and slipped out five peas. Suppose she had to tell her mother what she was thinking about? The smile lingered —through the trees she could see the turn in the brook. Regarding her—the slim, slightly stooping girl, hands dreaming over the green pods—"Oh, well," said Mrs. Kellogg, helplessly; she had a way of saying "Oh, well," either before jelly which would not jell or before other manifestations of life she could not control. But as she examined her jelly, finding it had done what it should, she said briskly: "Why, Rosie would have had those peas shelled long ago."

Naomi laughed. Of course Rosie would have had them shelled. What did Rosie—twelve—have to think about? But now Naomi's fingers began to move—fingers running, fingers running a race.

Peas danced into the dish, pods fell upon other pods. She wanted a bath before supper, get that petticoat ironed for her blue dress. The last thing she would put on the blue dress—they would not know.

At thought of their not knowing, as if to make up for something, she talked pleasantly with her mother of how Willie, her little brother, seven, had disappeared from sight with the brook. He and the Sears boy were playing tramp. Said they were going to play begging at houses.

"Goodness!" exclaimed Annie Kellogg. "Hope they don't beg at Maria Copeland's!"

"Oh," said Naomi, shocked. "Oh, I guess they won't do that!"

"No," her mother agreed, rather grimly, "I guess not."

Naomi looked at her mother. No, people didn't beg at Mrs. Copeland's—didn't even play begging. Not Kelloggs. Well, *she* didn't beg there. She didn't have to!

"What," she began guardedly, "what *is* it about Mrs. Copeland?"

"Oh, she's queer," her mother said. "Stand-of-fish. Always was. Thinks she's better than other folks."

"Of course," said Naomi. As if she didn't know that! "But why?"

"Why? How do I know why?"

A shadow moved across the sunlight on the pods. A man was moving across the yard. Caleb Evans stood in the door.

Oh, dear! Now her mother would ask him to stay for supper!

"Well, well—*Caleb.*" Her mother was shaking hands. "So you got back!"

"Yes, I got back," he said, in his high voice which sometimes made it hard to keep from laughing when he prayed in church. He held out a limp hand to Naomi. As it was in this fashion he shook hands with her, how did he manage to shake hands with her mother at all?

"Well, Naomi,"—with Caleb the *mi* of her name became a squeak. "See your mother manages to keep you busy."

"That's right," she said, and looked down at her work, for his eyes were too glad to see her, eyes too small to be that glad.

"Now you just make yourself at home, Caleb. Mr. Kellogg'll be up from the meadow. And I'll whip up some baking-powder biscuits for supper. Maybe you've not had them out in Colorado. And just yesterday 'Omi made a chocolate cake."

"Well, say—guess I'm in luck," said Caleb, and Naomi had to act as if he had said something.

They had missed him at church, Mrs. Kellogg told him. Brother Baldwin said Sunday, in meet-

ing, he hoped they would soon have Brother Caleb
Evans with them again.

"*Well*—" Caleb began.

"Don't tell me you're going for good!" cried
Naomi's mother.

Caleb crossed his knees. "Mrs. Kellogg," he
said, a little unsteady with importance, "I have
come home to sell my store," and he looked at
Naomi.

Now she was pleasanter to him. What would he
do out there?

He told of the land he had taken. It was a
mountain valley. Well, they called it a valley, he
laughed. It was miles and miles long—'most a
hundred, and wide too, the shape of a big meat
platter it was, and shut in by mountains—bigger
than you had seen in pictures, even; snow on them
all the year.

"Goodness!" cried Mrs. Kellogg, "what a place
to live!"

A great place to live, Caleb insisted, and talked
of the new irrigation system, potatoes as big as
turnips. Naomi's father came up from the meadow,
and Caleb told him about farming in Colorado.
"It's pretty too," he said, looking Naomi's way;
"flowers grow wild just like the grass. And at
sundown, as the sun goes down in the west, it's the
mountains to the eastward are red as blood."

"Now, *Caleb*," protested Mrs. Kellogg, teasing

him the way they all teased one another at church sociables.

Caleb liked his new land. He wasn't so bad when he talked about it. At supper Naomi even asked him questions.

"I never heard Caleb talk so much," her mother said as they cleared the table after Caleb had gone out to the barn with Mr. Kellogg.

"No," Naomi agreed cordially, "he was quite interesting, wasn't he?"

But now she wanted him to go. She'd have to wear her white skirt—she had wanted the blue sateen! And how would she get away by half-past eight? She didn't want to keep Joe waiting, and —why, it seemed she couldn't live if she didn't see him to-night! Shaking the tablecloth in the doorway, she stood looking up the brook. Her father and Caleb were examining the new mower. Caleb had a hardware store at their edge of town; he was supposed to know something about machinery. But would he go home now?

"I'll have to study to-night," she told her mother, firmly. Naomi was going to summer Normal.

"You must visit with Caleb a while first."

"He's visiting with Father," and indeed it was always a question whether Caleb came to see Naomi or Naomi's parents. He was much nearer her age than theirs, but he was such a "worker in the church" it seemed to put him in their generation.

"Your father'll want to go to bed. Now you be nice to Caleb, Naomi, his first night home. He's such a good man," she added, piously; and when her mother took that tone it seemed a little insincere, though no reason why it should. "My, how he will be missed in the church!"

Being nice to him—that of course was all that would come of it, and her mother really wouldn't want more to come of it—Caleb looking like this; though it wasn't so much the way he looked, as the way he *was*. He made her think of some one in a silly play, pretending to be alive, and not being funny about it. Even people who knew less about things than her mother and father would know that a girl who had gone around some with Joe Copeland never could be anything but nice to Caleb Evans.

She went into her room to comb her hair, and, pulling it down the way Joe said made her beautiful, she smiled to think how much better she knew him than any one suspected, how much more it was than going around some. But here she was both happy and troubled; it seemed so silly not to go around with him the way other couples went together when they were in love. What was the matter with Joe's mother, anyway? She'd better get over her silly, old-fashioned notions. This was 1888! Joe was twenty-one. Did she expect him to be tied to her all his life? And why didn't Joe tell her, once and

for all? Well, he would soon. Very soon now.
Then what would her own mother and father think
—when they knew it had kept on unknown to them?

Naomi's father thought he had stopped it. He
said the Copelands weren't any better than the Kelloggs, if they did have a bigger house and more land,
and if Maria Copeland wouldn't let her son go with
Naomi openly—this after Joe, much embarrassed,
came over to get out of taking her to a lawn social
where his mother would be—then Joe Copeland
needn't think he could sneak over and sit in the
Kelloggs' parlor. So they didn't sit in the parlor.
They sat by the brook.

In the yard she heard her father say "Copeland,"
and stood by the open window as he told Caleb
about a wonderful new haying machine they had at
the Copelands'. He had seen it to-day from the
meadow. First one of its kind around there.

"Naomi," called her mother, in undertone,
"they're coming in now."

On the porch her mother told the news of the
church, then went inside to see that Rosie really
went to bed, instead of just pretending. Her father
yawned and yawned, finally said, "Well, I was up at
five this morning. I'll be up at five to-morrow.
Guess I'll leave you young folks to entertain your-
selves." He laughed as though this were a joke, and
it did seem a joke—Caleb as young folks, and enter-

taining. Because it was too much like a joke she was nice to Caleb at first, telling him about Normal.

It became dark. Night was a friend now—inviting, sheltering. Nice sound in the trees to-night, and through them she saw the stars. She could hear the brook, singing in the bigger music of the trees, the brook which came from the Copeland place and ran through theirs, into which Joe told her he whispered messages for her. Joe was like that. Joe was her lover—all through her went this message, as she watched the thin, uncertainly moving shoulders of Caleb Evans, on whose neck fell the light from the hall. He should have moved out of the light.

Soon now Joe would be leaving home for the turn in the brook, that secret place where it was hidden from the Copeland house and from the Kelloggs'. He would be sitting there, perhaps lying flat on the grass beside the water. He would spring to his feet, his arms around her. "Naomi!" he would whisper. "Naomi!" There together—just them— and as if everything around them were their friend. The brook—

"It's the country of the future," Caleb was saying in his high voice. "If the branch railroad . . ."

When she had a chance she said, "The worst thing about Normal is that we have to study so hard. Why, we have to study at night."

"You do?" said Caleb, not paying much attention. He pulled a long grass beside the step and began splitting it down its length. "I'll be going out there in about two months now." He jerked the blade of grass in two. "How'd you like to go with me?" he asked, a little giving her the feeling this was a joke at a church sociable.

"Oh, I couldn't go so far from home," she answered, with a laugh.

"We would make a new home." No, not a joke now. He was proposing to her!

"Thank you, Caleb," she said. "It is not possible," she added primly, saying within herself, "Well, I should think not!"

"It's not so lonely out there as you might think," he went on, argumentatively, the way she had heard him argue in meeting. "There's young folks in the town. My land's only three miles out. You'd have your own horse and buggy."

"You'll find some nice girl right there in that town, Caleb," she said gently.

"It's you I want!" And as he looked up at her she wanted to move away from him, for she saw he did want her, and that kind of wanting was between her and Joe.

But it gave her a chance to get away. She rose and said with dignity: "I am sorry, but I do not feel that way, Caleb. And if you will excuse me, I will really have to do my studying now."

CHAPTER II

"*P*ROPOSED to you? You, *you*, Naomi?"
Laughing ardent eyes on her upturned face, Joe's low rich lazy voice—lover's voice—his warm low laugh, here by the brook, the world asleep—not knowing—alone here together, this freshness in the trees above the sweet sound of the clear brook, the far-away gentle stars. Oh, she was happy now, as Joe held her and they laughed together.

He held her a little away from him. "But you haven't told me. Did you accept him, Naomi?" He bent her back and bent over her. "Did you accept him, Naomi?" Again and again he asked it, low, excited—Joe, her lover.

"See the stars in the brook," she said, later, as she pinned back her hair.

"No," said Joe, "I see the stars in your eyes."

The breeze brought the smell of drying grass, hay her father had worked with that afternoon. "Why, it's like something human," Joe was telling her, about their new haying machine. "It's got teeth and jaws; it's got long arms that can lift a whole load of hay and know just what to do with it. Wouldn't surprise me a bit to have it say Hello!"

They laughed. It was as easy for them to laugh as for the brook. They would be through the haying soon now, Joe said.

She turned her face to him, that beauty of one who has been ardently loved, rarefied by the starlight, and by a wistfulness.

He understood, and took her hands, as in pledge. "Yes, Naomi. Just as I told you."

When the Copeland fields had once more been harvested Joe was to tell his mother he was going to marry Naomi Kellogg.

"Why—" she began hesitatingly, she would be happier if they could talk of it, if Joe and his mother were not something shut away from Joe and Naomi. "Why is it, Joe?"

"Why is what?" he asked; but she knew he understood, for he was a little away from her now, making her feel just a little as his mother made one feel.

"Why is it your mother doesn't like me?"

"Oh, it isn't you she doesn't like, Naomi. She doesn't want me to like you."

"Yes, but why?"

"How do I know why?" he said—that was what her mother had said about Mrs. Copeland. "Maybe she's jealous."

They laughed; but the laugh did not bring them together.

"You see Father died so long ago. And me the only child. Our house isn't like your house, Naomi. I like your house—kind of free and easy, people saying what they think instead of—not saying what they think," he finished uncertainly. "Mother— she's kept too much by herself. What she feels she keeps shut up inside herself. Has for years."

"And she thinks she's better than we are," Naomi thought. Things were done just right at the Copelands'. Naomi used to be there at times, before there was this trouble about her and Joe going together. Everything was where it belonged. But it all smelled too clean. Mrs. Copeland's eyes kept you from feeling comfortable in her clean house, as if she were shutting herself away while she looked at you, as if she were afraid you might touch her. So many things you just wouldn't think of talking about to her. But Naomi wished Joe weren't afraid of his mother.

As if suspecting she had moved a little away from him, he put his arms around her, to keep her from going away, and knowing it could keep her.

"You do love me, Joe? You do love me?"

"I do love you, Naomi," he whispered.

She knew it was true, and this love made all the world different.

"I must be going," she had said, but could not bear to leave him, wanting to hold, that she might carry it with her, this feeling of love making all the world different. She lay flat, eyes closed, Joe sitting beside her, but not touching her now, as if each would feel alone what it was they had together. She smelled her father's hay from the field across the brook; her hand was on moss deeper and smoother than velvet; the trees were a large fresh sound, like something going over the world; the brook was tender and clear. She opened her eyes and looked up at the stars.

"Why do people ever sleep at night?" she laughed. Yet sleep was sweet in her now—her legs, her breasts, wanted sleep here where the smell of the hay came across the brook, and the great trees said —Sleep.

"No," she exclaimed, sitting up. "I mustn't."

They walked by the brook until almost in sight of the Kelloggs'. Then he held her close, murmuring: "Naomi!"

"Some day we will not have to part," she said.

"Soon we will be together—for all the days and all the nights," he answered; and they held each other's hands in wonder at this.

"Good-night, my Joe."

"Good-night, darling Naomi."

CHAPTER III

THE Copeland farm was on the main road, about four miles out from town. Just as you reached the edge of their land you took the branch road that curved round the Copeland place, dipped a little, and took you to the Kelloggs'; the places joined, though they were on different roads. The farms sat back to back, and the brook ran through both.

You did not see the Copeland house from the Kelloggs', but you saw it on the main road, just before you turned off. Naomi was looking at it now, driving home from town with three other girls who went to Normal. A proud-looking white house with green shutters. It was on a slight rise, which made its two stories and attic even higher than they were; most of the farmhouses, like the Kelloggs', was story and a half. This house had only a stoop, not a porch. It did not invite you to enter. It looked too big for a widow and her son; perhaps it was this made it bleak, though so well kept up. There were formal little trees, unlike other trees around here, and not friendly. Mrs. Copeland was outside, talking to a man working at the fence, though not really talking to him, it seemed, but pointing. She was more erect than Naomi's mother.

The buggy stopped at the turn, the other girls continued along the highway, and Naomi walked toward home. She had not felt like talking, for her own thoughts were big—sweet—within her, so it was good to be alone. And she liked their road— this narrow dirt road, trees all along it, clover and other flowers growing in the grass. To the right was Copeland land, most of the time shut off from her by a long low hill that was like a wave, but to the left she could see for miles—all the farms between here and town, flat stretches and then gently rolling country. Illinois. Beautiful Illinois! Black plowed fields and green fields of grain, cows in pasture, and in far meadows horses hauling great loads. Here and there moved farm machinery, like some impossible kind of beast. All the country was at work, and there was a light on it to-day—this late afternoon of white clouds which moved swiftly— a light that made the whole of it seem beautiful, as —as love makes all different, and beautiful.

There was a break in the wave that was the hill which edged the Copeland place; looking up this dip she saw what looked like a monster with many arms and legs. The men around it looked small. Joe came running toward it, throwing up his arms as in excited salute to the machine. He bent down and began showing the men something. How strong—with what swift sureness he moved! The creature made a great weary gesture that took the hay far around it, threw it high, held it in arms sent out to receive it. Joe, his back to her, threw back his head with a laugh. ("Wouldn't surprise me a bit to have it say Hello!")

She walked slowly—watching him, those movements she knew, as he dominated the men around him, dominated the machine; behind him the shadow of the hills, he in the sunlight—working his own land. Power he had—laughing power. "Goodnight, darling Naomi,"—that was what he had said.

William Kellogg looked up from the hay he was stacking and saw his daughter coming, swinging her bag of books. There was a wreath of flowers on her straw hat, and her pink dress was ruffled.

"Hello, Nomi," he called with pleasure, and walked over to the fence to talk with her. "Well, did you learn anything to-day?" for Naomi and her father were on good terms, in spite of this trouble about Joe Copeland. Her father was jolly and kind, though famous for his temper, and fervent in everything having to do with the Bible and church.

"You want to go home with Nomi, Patsy?" he said to the curly brown water spaniel who had come running after him.

"Go with Nomi," he urged, just because he knew so well Patsy would stay with him.

Naomi laughed. Father was nice about Patsy.

For years now they had been chums. If Patsy were left home he would sit on the gatepost and, trembling, watch for his master to come in sight. Then a leap, a wild yapping, a racing down the road. "Father's coming," they would say in the house; and even though Father and his horse Lady were almost home, they would draw up for Pat to get in, that he might ride into the barn sitting proudly on the seat.

The brook was saying things about last night. The thrush was singing in the elm.

The trees before the Kelloggs' were great trees, and that made the house seem even lower than it was. How nice and shady it looked in there; how cool the brook sounded!

"That you, Naomi?" her mother called from the kitchen.

The cherries her mother was putting up were rich red—the look of them like the feel of the moss on which her hand had rested the night before. The branches near the window swept shadow across the sunlight that made the cherries sing with color.

Her mother looked tired. "I'll help you with supper," Naomi said.

"You rest a while first, dear. Was it hot in town?"

She went in her room—a downstairs room, back of the dining-room, in the ell of the house. It was this made it easy to go out and meet Joe after the others had gone upstairs. She liked her downstairs room, where she could lean out the window and feel the freshness coming up from the grass. She liked walking very late in the night and feeling near the brook, when all the others were asleep. Joe heard the brook from his room, too.

Yes, she must help Mother. When she came in the kitchen she had noticed how much more stooped her mother was than Mrs. Copeland. Mrs. Copeland had worked too, but she could hold herself like that because she had always held away from people. "Oh—well," she could hear her mother saying now, as Rosie told how Willie had broken the big pink geranium, jumping out the window after the Sears boy.

She looked in the glass as she took off her hat and made her hair come down over her forehead. She frowned, for she was tired now; not one of the times she looked beautiful. Sometimes she did —sometimes not. But as she unfastened the dress she was about to take off, put her arms behind her head, stretching, then her throat, her head thrown back, looking at herself with half-closed eyes—it had come back. It went, but quickly came back, that which made her beautiful. She took out Joe's picture—she had put it away when they said he couldn't come to the house any more. If it was all to be secret, then the picture should be secret too. She looked at Joe—down into the smile of the picture—not a smile, but about to smile—into the deep eyes, then again looked at herself in the mirror. She flushed—her dress all open like this.

Mother had said rest a little first, and she was tired, for it had been late when she got in the night before. She lay down on the big walnut bed. Her room was nice this hour in the afternoon. She liked the pink rosebuds of the wallpaper. The room was so much cooler, pleasanter to be in, since she had taken up the carpet and painted the floor gray, like the girls in town who had gone to college.

She turned the pages of a magazine. Italy. It was a land of romance. Terraced hillsides. Orange groves, vineyards and the olive-trees. They were lovers, the Italians. Love was in their eyes, their voices; centuries they had sung songs of love, fought and died for it. The nightingale. Venice. Murmuring of water and the ardent whisperings.

The magazine lay under her hand; drowsily she thought of Italy, a land of romance. The perfume of roses came in through her window; there was that good smell of drying hay—full clear song of the thrush. The water of the brook—waters of Venice. Ardent whispers through the centuries. She was close to Joe. His eyes were loving her. His voice whispered. . . .

She sat up. Through her waking dream came running footsteps. Her father's voice—excited, low: "Annie! Annie!" Her father telling something in the kitchen. From her mother a sound that made her afraid.

She went from her room to the dining-room, stood by the open door of the kitchen. Their backs were turned. Her father was making movements with his hands. "He was showing them how it worked. He must have done the wrong thing— for like this they came up—them iron teeth like a lion's teeth! They went into his bowels like he was—"

"Oh!" cried Mrs. Kellogg, her hands pressed over her mouth. "Oh! Oh! Oh!"

"And the great beam descended upon him—"

"*Who—?*" shrieked Naomi.

"Oh—oh, my darling!" Her mother ran toward her.

She held her mother away and faced her father. "*Who?*"

"Yes, Naomi—him."

"Not—not—?"

"Yes—Joe."

"Hurt?" she whispered. "You mean—he's hurt?"

"I mean—he's dead, daughter."

CHAPTER IV

THE leaves had turned red, but Naomi had not seen them this year. The thrush had gone, the brook was stronger. If she missed or heard these sounds she did not know she missed or heard them. "They've finished the last grain at the Copelands'," her father said at dinner that day. She rose and came to her room. "William," her mother admonished. "She ought to be getting hold of herself by now," her father replied.

The Copeland fields had been harvested. And when this grain had been gathered she and Joe were to have been married. She sat looking at Joe's picture.

Later her mother came in. "Caleb Evans is out here, dear. Won't you come speak to him?"

"Oh, Mother—please. Don't ask me, please!"

So desperate was the tone Annie Kellogg sat down, looking at her daughter, more and more troubled. At the first they had accepted that Joe's death would be a shock to Naomi. She and Joe had kept company not so long before; it seemed she had gone on being fond of him. Perhaps—poor Naomi—she had hoped it would one day be different. But as the summer progressed, Naomi remaining white and strange, not speaking and scarcely eating or sleeping, then her mother had tried to reason with her. "You must make yourself think of other things now, Naomi. It was a shock, but it isn't," she had put it gently as she could, "as if you and Joe had been engaged. You had stopped keeping company, you know. It—it doesn't seem right you should grieve like this. You must go around with the girls like you always did, or people will be talking."

Naomi would not reply, holding her hands tight together, looking away.

It was to her father she told something of the truth. Coming along outside her room he had one day heard her crying and gone in to her. "You're letting yourself run down. And—well, Joe did give you up, didn't he, Naomi?"

"Joe never gave me up!" she flashed. "We loved each other. We were going to be married in the fall."

Her father had not known what to say.

Now her mother was saying: "I think it would be a good thing for you to talk to Caleb, even if you don't want to. Sometimes we have to force ourselves to do things. Even people who have been married to each other have to bear these partings. Think how much worse it would be if—"

Naomi raised her eyes and looked at her mother,

and the mother could not go on, though she did not know why she could not.

Fearing she would be forced to go out and talk with Caleb Evans about having sold his store, Naomi slipped out the back door, around the barn, quickly into the trees and up the brook.

She went alone where she had gone to meet Joe.

It was not the first time she had come here alone. In those nights of midsummer, the family asleep upstairs, she would get up and go as if to meet her lover, as if the life in her that had been stopped, not knowing what had happened, must go through the summer night to fulfillment. Sometimes not knowing what she was doing, sometimes pretending she would find him there, her feet would follow the way they knew, and she would wait by the brook. One night she had been unable to bear the silence, ran around calling to him; that night she lay flat in the brook, reaching out for him, calling his name until the water choked her, and she had gone home sobbing, "Joe—Joe!"

But now she sat very still where she and Joe had lain, her hand on the moss, leaves falling into the brook. Joe. Where was Joe? How could it be that they had been as they had, and that he could go and she be left here to know alone what they had known together? What would she do? How could she live in a world where Joe was not?

It was hard for her to rise. She felt clumsy.

She seemed to grow heavier lately, even though she ate so little. Suddenly she put her hand on the tree. What was this strange feeling?

She had not thought about things, fears had not come to her. That in her which thought and feared was not alive. But now, for the first time, she considered. The months had gone by. Could —would it be *possible?* No—of course not; such things did not happen—not really, not to one's self. But again, more strongly, that feeling unlike anything she had known. Here by the brook where they had been lovers, Joe's child moved within her.

CHAPTER V

IT was shorter to go across fields to the Copelands', following the brook. But that did not
seem the way to go to-day. She had dressed
carefully, soberly, and it was with a great serious-
ness, and formally, that she walked around the curve
from their house to the house that had been Joe's
home. "I will take a little walk," she had said to her
mother. "Oh, I'm so glad!" her mother cried, for
she had tried in vain to get Naomi to go and see
some of the girls. "Want Rosie to go with you?"

"No, Mother."

"Don't you want to take Patsy?"

"No, Mother."

How quiet she was, and as if she were far away.
Mrs. Kellogg followed to the porch. A November
wind that got to the bone. "This isn't such a good
day for a walk. 'Fraid maybe it's going to rain."

"Good-by, Mother," Naomi answered. She
wore her gloves. She had her handkerchief in her
hand, as if she were going to church. She walked
slowly.

Some of the shutters were closed at the Copelands'. The formal little trees looked dismal. She
stood a long time on the stoop after she had pulled

the bell. What would she do if Mrs. Copeland did not come to the door? Could she go to the back door? It did not seem she could.

Finally a cousin who had been staying there opened the door a little way.

"I have come to see Mrs. Copeland," said Naomi.

"She doesn't see people much now," replied this woman uncertainly.

"I know. But this is something important."

"You are—?"

"I am Naomi Kellogg."

"Oh, yes—one of the neighbors' girls."

"Yes. Come about something very important."

The door opened wider, Naomi stepped in.

"Well, I'll *see*," said the tall, thin woman, Joe's "old maid cousin." Again she seemed uncertain, but said, "You can just step in the parlor."

In the cold parlor Naomi sat on the edge of a horsehair chair. On the center table was a picture of Joe, the same picture she had.

As she sat looking at it some one stepped into the room. It was the cousin again. "Mrs. Copeland can't see you."

Naomi rose. "Tell her it is something about Joe. Tell her—it is something she must know."

She sat looking at the picture. Then Joe's mother stood in the doorway.

She was much older, and yet she was not different. She had withered, but it was herself was there, withered. At first Naomi was sorry for her. That made it easier to tell what she had come to tell, for she had come bringing her something. She was not afraid; indeed, from the moment, late in the night, when she saw what she must do, she had not been afraid.

Mrs. Copeland did not speak, did not sit down, so Naomi, too, remained standing. "It is about Joe," she said.

Joe's mother, though as if a light had changed on her, more gray, stood there in that way she had, as if you would not dare to touch her.

"You did not want us to—keep company," Naomi began.

Mrs. Copeland pulled herself a little higher, though it was not as easy as it had been.

"But we did," said Naomi. "We went on seeing each other. By the brook—when you were asleep."

What was going to happen? Looking at Mrs. Copeland you knew that anything could happen now. But she herself did not know what was going to happen, she did not know what to do. Perhaps she did not know what to do because in all her life no one had spoken to her like that, because until this moment people had obeyed that manner which said you could not come near her. Now Naomi had to come near her.

"We went on seeing each other, because we loved each other." She halted, unable to say anything else because she must say this. "Why did you think you could stop love?"

The old woman trying to be Mrs. Copeland took a step backward. "No," said Naomi, "you cannot go away from this."

But because she looked like that—Joe's mother, the mother Joe loved, though afraid of, Naomi went to her and pulled up a chair. "Oh, please sit down," she said.

Mrs. Copeland sank to the chair. She had to. Naomi, too, sat down. "I do not come to make it harder for you. I come—bringing you something."

Yet when she came right to it, it seemed she could not tell it.

"Joe is not dead," she began at last. "Not—all of him. Not—really.

"Oh, don't you *see*," she cried, as Joe's mother just sat there, "we loved each other so much—by the brook—in the summer nights—" A silence. Naomi said, low: "Joe has left a child."

It seemed a long time that neither of them moved; so big it was, this thing right there between them.

Suddenly Mrs. Copeland's face began to work. "You *trollop!*" It was as if she had spit the word.

Naomi could not believe what she saw and heard.

"I thought you would be glad," was all she could say.

"*Glad!*" Her clenched hands moved as if her body had lost control of them. "Glad to know my son deceived me and left a bastard to besmirch our name!"

"But it is Joe's child," whispered Naomi.

The ugly old woman grew suddenly shrewd. "How do I know that? How's there any telling—with loose women like you?"

"What did you say?" asked Naomi, bewildered.

Mrs. Copeland got to her feet. "It's money you want, I suppose. Here to blackmail me, are you?" She clenched her hands and shook them. "I'll have the police on you! Coming into my own house and—" She had raised her voice and her cousin came hurrying in.

"Oh—oh, Maria, what is it? Now, you mustn't— What have you *done* to her?" she demanded of Naomi.

But as the woman sought to support her, Mrs. Copeland came into her old manner of command. Pointing to the door she said: "Put that woman out of my house!"

So Naomi went out from the place that had been Joe's home. "I thought she would be glad," she would say within herself, sobbing under her breath.

CHAPTER VI

NOW she was afraid and did not want to be alone in her room, but wanted to be near her mother and father, even near Rosie and Willie, and Patsy. She would follow them from dining-room to kitchen. She got some sewing and sat by the kitchen stove, across from her father, who was figuring in his notebook. Then he read in the Bible, as was his custom before going to bed. He wondered how this could be—that God knew about every one of us. Her father believed everything in the Bible was just as it said it was, and often he sat by the kitchen stove, wondering about things. Jesus must have been lonely on earth, he thought.

Her mother remained downstairs after he had gone to bed. She was setting bread. Each time she was about to leave, Naomi would find a new thing to talk about—the missionary society, anything would do. She wanted to hear her mother's voice, to feel usual things going on around her.

She was afraid downstairs after it grew still above. She wanted to wake Rosie and get her to come down and sleep with her, but feared this would seem strange. In the dark she lay wondering what

she would do. She would have to tell her mother
and father now. It would be what is called a disgrace. Perhaps she ought to go away; but she
pulled the covers more closely around her. She
could not go away—not now; not all by herself,
to some strange place.

Words Mrs. Copeland had said were like something crawling on her. Strange she had not herself
thought it that way—the shame. But she and Joe,
it had come to seem what should be; and now, that
a child should be coming, after Joe had gone—to
be born after he was dead—this had been as a
miracle she must share with the woman who
mourned for Joe.

Now she saw what every one would see. Well,
she would not expect people to have anything to
do with her. She would just stay here at home,
help them all. Yes, she would work for every one
of them. People would not hold it against the rest
of the family—not much, not for long. Here at
home they would be good to her, would let her stay
close to them.

Rains had swollen the brook. A more powerful
stream than the brook which knew her and Joe.
And yet, the same brook—something that had been
then, was now. Something that went on. Something that went on after Joe had stopped; would
go on when she herself was no more. When at last

she grew sleepy the brook had become the child within her—going on—on—summer nights—wild rains and winter. Then spring again—sweet earth of summer.

When she saw her father come into the yard the next afternoon she knew she would not have to tell them. Once before she had seen him move like that. His horse had broken loose and run home. He came running after with the whip. Oh, she could not believe it—years after, she would try to forget it—that it was her father who jumped up and down and lashed his horse like that.

He rushed through the kitchen and into her room.

"Been lying around with Joe Copeland, have you? And now you're left with his bastard! That's it, is it? All right, young lady! Oh, all *right,* young lady—" He began creeping up on her.

"Mother!" screamed Naomi.

Her mother was holding her away from her father. "William!" she cried, holding up her hand to stay the man who stood there as if about to leap. "Have you gone crazy? What's happened? What *is* the matter?"

"Ask *her*—what's the matter. No, you don't have to *ask* her. Look at her! Yes—there! *Look* at her."

Naomi, cowering, face turned away—one saw the woman who would have a child.

"What do you mean?" whispered the mother, quick, faint.

"Joe Copeland. Sneakin' out nights to him. A Kellogg lying down in the grass for a Copeland!"

"That's not true! Naomi! It isn't—"

"Ask Maria Copeland if it's true!"

"Maria Copeland! Does *she* know?" breathed Mrs. Kellogg.

"Askin' help from the mother of the boy who'd wronged her."

Then Naomi stood straight. "I did *not* ask help!" She strove to cease crying so she could say it. "I thought she would be glad."

"Glad?" cried Mrs. Kellogg. "Oh—*glad,*" she repeated, sinking down on Naomi's bed, covering her face, sobbing: "Oh, how will we ever hold up our heads again!"

The father pointed to the mother who cowered there. "You see, do you? See what you've done to the mother that loved you and worked for you?"

Now he saw Joe's picture on the table by Naomi's bed. He sprang to it. "Not in this house!" he cried, and before Naomi could struggle with him he had torn it—again—again. In a fury because this was all of Joe he could reach he would spit upon it, crying: "There—take that! Now, take that!" shoving Naomi aside as she came near him.

But at last she beat against him with her fists. "You stop that or I'll kill you! You let Joe alone!"

And as he spat again she kicked at her father. Her mother sprang from the bed commanding: "Here. Stop it now, both of you!" The father fell back and Naomi sank sobbing to the floor, gathering up the defiled fragments, crying: "O Joe—help me! Come back to me. Help me!" until at last from deep sobs her father cried: "Have mercy upon us! O God, have mercy!"

CHAPTER VII

SO this was what had come of that beauty.
It was here she could not understand. Remembering the summer nights when she had
been, not only happy, but as if let in where all
goodness and beauty were hers, remembering, not
alone mad love, but moments of gentle goodness—
moments clear and pure as the sound of the brook,
remembering the stars in the water, the trees over-
head, smell of the hay her father had cut coming
to them through the great still fresh night, remembering what went on in her heart as she heard the
thrush—that the beauty which breathed in the summer could lead to what happened in her room
yesterday— "I must be stupid," she told herself.
"Something has happened to my mind. I am not
seeing things the way other people see them."

"Nomi!" called her little brother. "Come look
what Patsy can do! Nomi! See Patsy sit on his
hind legs and hold the stick!"

Her eyes were suddenly hot and wet—that her
little brother should call her to play with the dog,
as if nothing had happened, as if she were a person
who could come and play with the dog. "You let

that dog alone!" her father roughly commanded Willie.

Her father just sat in the kitchen, his head bent, thinking. Her mother, eyes red, walked about softly, as if some one were dead.

She came in Naomi's room now, bringing clothes she had ironed. "Here are your things—dear." She lay them on the bed, turned away, crying.

Naomi went to her and awkwardly put a hand on the stooping shoulder. "I'm sorry, Mother."

"Oh, Naomi—weren't we good to you? Weren't we always good to you?"

"Why, yes, Mother—of course. What—what has that to do with it?"

"What's it to do with it?" her mother demanded sharply, through her tears. "Oh, that you—*you*, Naomi, should disgrace us like this!"

Was there anything she could say? It seemed not, as if she and her mother were so far apart they could not now touch each other. Was there no way to—reach?

"Mother,"—it was so Naomi tried to reach— "Joe and I loved each other. Don't you—remember, Mother. Isn't there—isn't there anything for you to *remember?* It wasn't—the way Father talked yesterday. It was—so different," was all she could say.

A pause—not hostile. Then, "Well, I don't know what we're going to do," her mother said, helplessly. "Your father can't think—what to do."

"I'll go away," Naomi said wearily.

Her mother looked up quickly. "No—no, Naomi; you're not to do anything at all. Promise me you won't. Not till we—decide."

But of course that was what she would have to do.

When her father went out of the house she would go and help her mother. She and her father tried not to see each other. He made her feel ashamed, as if she were showing herself in some vile way.

He went to town the next afternoon, and when he came back he called his wife upstairs. Naomi heard low voices.

At supper her father was different—very quiet, but as she had seen him in church when the minister preached a sermon that moved him.

Her mother made the children go to bed early, and herself went upstairs. Then her father called her into the kitchen.

"Sit down, Naomi," he said.

"Daughter, something has happened for which you must all your days thank God. You must love your Maker and serve Him. He has saved you, Naomi, and saved us all." Naomi waited. Her father said: "Caleb will marry you."

CHAPTER VIII

CALEB EVANS sat at the table with them, and she sat next to Caleb. There was the manner of a Sunday dinner, though it was not Sunday. "Will you have the butter, Naomi?" Caleb would ask her, with consideration. They treated him as if he had done some noble thing in the church; and he himself had that manner.

Mrs. Copeland had said Naomi must be got away from there. The Kelloggs did not know what was the right thing to do. Perhaps it was a matter to take up with Brother Baldwin.

Caleb Evans had come to the parsonage to turn over church accounts, for he was about to leave for Colorado, and Mr. Kellogg, who had broken down when the minister took the matter in prayer to God, told Caleb about Joe Copeland and Naomi. After the three men had sat there for a time, "I will marry Naomi and take her with me to Santa Clara," Caleb said. They could scarcely believe what it was they heard. Never had they known so grand a Christian act. "God will bless and reward you," the minister said as he shook hands with Caleb. And so there was over them all the manner of a great deed being done, and toward

Naomi a certain exalted tenderness, for it was upon her this goodness was bestowed. Only Naomi herself did not partake of the quality of this fervor. When she heard Caleb's voice she knew only she would not again hear Joe's voice, and when he turned his small eyes upon her she wanted to run away, for it was not alone the light of Christian charity she saw there.

This was a Tuesday, and she and Caleb would be married Thursday and leave at once for Colorado. Mrs. Kellogg was busy getting ready Naomi's things; Naomi, as one stunned, was little help to her mother.

Rosie was being punished. "Naomi's getting fat!" she had cried when, making conversation at table, they spoke of the increasing bulk of old Mrs. Sloane. "Go to your room!" her father commanded. "What was so bad about that?" Rosie asked as Naomi came up with some pudding for her sister.

"Are you honest going to marry Caleb Evans, Nomi?"

"Yes," said Naomi.

"I always thought he was kind of funny-looking."

"Yes," Naomi agreed.

"Well, why do you marry him, then? Why don't you stay here at home with us?"

So much did she want to stay at home with them that she had to hurry from Rosie's room.

Caleb took her hand as he said good-by. She could not bear the feel of his hand around hers. "Brother Baldwin and I will be here on Thursday, Naomi," he said, as if it were a promise, fervor in his small pale eyes. "Good-by, then, Caleb," said her father, shaking hands with him a long time. "Until Thursday," and her father's voice was unsteady with feeling.

"Now, Naomi, we'll just look through the things in these drawers," her mother said briskly.

"It will be interesting out there in the new country," her mother began determinedly, after they had worked in silence. "It is hard for us to have you go so far away; but, oh, my dear—how *good* he is! Think what it means to us all! I can hardly believe it is true!"

"No," said Naomi.

She was taking things from the table where Joe's picture had stood. Even the picture of him was gone. She closed her eyes and tried to make the picture of Joe, but in between came the picture of Caleb Evans. "Oh!" she cried. "No!"

Her mother, bent over the sheets Naomi would take, rose and came to her. "Now, dear, you must just stop all foolishness. This—this will be over soon—your trouble. Caleb will give your child a home. He will let the world think it is his child— oh, how *good* he is! I never, never heard of such a thing! I wouldn't have believed it! And you will make friends out there in the new country. There is a church—"

"Will I have to sleep with him?" Naomi asked.

"*Naomi!*" her mother protested in a low shocked tone.

"Will I?" Naomi demanded. "And—and everything?"

Mrs. Kellogg, red, confused, as one offended, replied that when you married a man you expected to be a wife to him. "And you, Naomi, it should be the endeavor of your whole life to be a good wife to him."

"*But you didn't tell me—did you accept him? Did you accept him, Naomi?*" Joe's voice, by the brook. She could hear the brook now, as she listened back into that night on the other side of summer, could hear, even through this November stream, the tender silvery brook of those early summer nights. But Joe's voice—low and rich with love, would not come again. Instead came Caleb's voice—high, in jerks. Joe was gone; even his picture was gone; and she *was* accepting Caleb Evans! It was like a dream that was becoming a nightmare.

"Mother!" she called, as she might call from a dream that threatened. "I do not think it is right for me to marry him, feeling as I do—about him; feeling as I do—about Joe."

"Brother Baldwin says it is right. There's to be no question about this, Naomi," she went on

sharply. "We have decided. It is the only thing
to *do*," she said, more weakly. "Think of Rosie.
What would we do about Rosie? Think what
people would *say*. Think of the life your child
would have. Yes, think of that, Naomi. Now get
your stockings out, dear. I want to see that they're
mended. This will be all right," she added soothingly, "once it's—over."

There was no use calling from this bad dream
to her mother. Her mother wanted to see that
the stockings were mended; she was loving about
many things, but she had no courage when it came
to what people would say. She knew what Naomi
was going into—what the bad dream would become, yet she went on talking cheerily about the
stockings, pretending she did not know.

Outside she heard Patsy's excited barking. Her
father was chopping wood. He would stop and
throw a chip for Patsy and Pat would return it and
demand it be thrown again. Watching her father,
she remembered things she understood better now
than she had at the time. A hired girl they had
once—so pretty; some of the lively pretty young
women in the church—even yet his eyes would follow them. She remembered things she had over-
heard when she was small and did not understand.
"*No*," her mother had said, fretfully, from their
room. Her father had wanted more love—she was
sure of that now. Perhaps he had these tempers

because he had wanted love and there had been so little in his life. Yes, that could be. Why, you felt like a different person—anything might happen —when a thing stood between you and what you wanted in love.

She put her cloak around her and went out where her father chopped wood beside the barn.

"Father," she said, "would you let me stay on here at home with you, instead of going away with Caleb Evans?"

He had looked up with feeling as he saw her coming toward him, had stopped his work to greet her, but now the kind look went.

"I am afraid," Naomi hurried on, "and—just a little longer, for now, for—this, I want to be here where I have always been. I walk around the house, and I do not want to leave the house; I want to lie in my own bed and look out the window into the trees. Out there I won't hear the brook." Her chin was quivering and he put his hand on her arm. At their feet Patsy, looking down at the chip, kept barking sharply. "I like to come in the kitchen and look around at the pans and things," she went on, sobs behind her words. "I never liked it so much before. Isn't my home my home, Father—in spite of everything? Can't I stay here a little longer?"

Yes, she had reached her father.

"I never needed you as much as I need you now." All this time Patsy was barking sharply and her father reached down and threw the stick for him. They watched him bringing it back—proudly, head high, as together they had so often watched him.

"But what could we do, Naomi?" her father asked. "Why, no," he added, rather crossly. "It would be disgrace. For you, for all of us."

"If you would—for my sake—stand a little disgrace?" she asked timidly. "Mostly it would be for just me. Then I would go away and make my living, and the living for my child. O Father, I would like that so much better!"

"And your child without a name?" He was getting excited. "There is a chance to give that child a name, and you should get down on your knees and thank God for it!"

"Father, do you remember, how it is—about love?"

He looked at her strangely.

"To live with Caleb Evans—loving Joe—"

The name brought his anger. "That was a *fine* love!"

"Yes," said Naomi, "it was a fine love. It was more beautiful than the most beautiful things in the world. It made everything else beautiful. The brook and the birds and the trees—each was its own music. I smelled the roses and the hay—the hay you cut was part of my love, Father. I felt the moss and saw the light move and the colors change. I felt the stillness and I loved you all—

Mother and you, and Rosie and Willie, Patsy, too, more than I ever loved you before. I felt *good*—good, Father. Goodness was beautiful to me, so beautiful I could cry when I thought of it."

There was a silence between father and daughter, and they were not far apart, as they stood out there by the chopping-block at the side of the barn, in the waning November day.

Yes, her father did know.

"Why, it wouldn't be right," said Naomi.

She should not have said that—"right."

"Brother Baldwin says it is right."

"Brother Baldwin—what does he know?"

"Now, see here, Naomi—" So it went into argument, into anger, and for one moment they had been close, and she knew that underneath it all, her father did understand.

Because he understood he covered it with talk about Caleb being a good man—why, a noble man he was; about God having been good to her, her child having a name. "You don't know what the world can be like, Naomi. A woman who hasn't her reputation—has nothing," he said piously. . . .

"First thing you know you'll be coming back home for a visit," he concluded in a voice he made almost jovial.

CHAPTER IX

NAOMI was dressed for going away. "A quarter of three. They will be here in a few minutes now," her mother said with her bright nervousness. Her father walked around in the shoes he wore to church, and they squeaked. There was an attempt to keep up conversation, as some people think conversations must be kept up at a funeral. Her father said: "Well, Naomi, it will be grand to see the mountains. You'll be the only member of the Kellogg family ever seen the mountains."

"Caleb says there is such a nice church," her mother would repeat. "Not our own denomination, but several of the denominations united."

"Well, that's a good idea, in a new country," her father would agree, and her parents would tell stories about churches uniting.

Naomi stooped down and put her hand on Patsy's head, felt his long silken ears. He looked up at her, wagging his tail. "Patsy," she said, low; but when she heard her own voice say "Patsy" she had to turn away. She looked from the window. The barn—the other sheds out there in the barnyard, rather tumble-down but so familiar—just as they always had been. Chickens scratching in the barn-yard, the cows standing on the other side of the bars. The lilac-bush, the roses, leaves shriveled now; the way the trees stood there, she saw them knowing she was going to see them forever just like this—each tree having its place among the other trees.

"I thought there was music at a wedding," said Rosie.

"Naomi is being married quietly at home, and going right away," said her mother, in a carefully comfortable voice.

"Doesn't there have to be a cake, with frosting, or candles, or something?"

"There is a cake. Afterwards we will have coffee and cake."

"With frosting?" demanded Willie.

"Be still!" roared his father.

Naomi went back into her own room. More of Joe seemed to be going now that she was leaving the room in which such great love of him, and grief for him, had been. She wished she could go too. She would rather lie still—unknowing—forever, than live with Caleb Evans. Why had she not done it, then? Why did she not do it now? As she stood there thinking of it, she was aware of her own heaviness. She could not kill that of Joe which lived.

The night before she got up and dressed to run

away. Where? To do what? She had no money. The night was dark. How would she get to town? She was afraid of the bulldog the Barnes let loose at night. These seemed little things; she ought to be able to go through them. But that in her which could drive ahead had died with Joe. And words Mrs. Copeland and her father had used—they were like rats. It came daylight and, worn out, she went to bed.

"There they come," said her mother in that voice which went with her best clothes.

Naomi was out the back door, into the trees and up the brook.

"Joe!" she whispered as she came to the sheltered place by the oak-tree. Sobbing, she sank down to the November earth. She was trying to make the picture of Joe's face, when she heard her father's voice—quick, subdued, angry: "Naomi! Naomi!"

"I am here, Father," she said, wearily.

"This is gratitude!" he cried, scarcely able to speak through his rage. "You come back and marry Caleb Evans or never again do you set foot in my house! An outcast you would be—a woman no decent person would open the door to! Come, Naomi," he said, suddenly natural, taking her arm. "This is foolishness. Come home now with me."

"Oh, Father—I can't!" Desperately she besought him now, with all her strength. "It's Joe! Joe! So long as I live—it will be Joe!"

"Joe is dead. And a fine thing you'd be doing for his memory!"

She looked at him.

"Haven't you thought of that? Now he's respected, mourned. You want to bring disgrace upon his grave? You want his name to be a byword as long as his name is remembered?"

Naomi stood there by the brook and thought.

"Father," she said, "I will go back and marry Caleb Evans, if you will do one thing for me."

"What am I to do for you, Naomi?" he asked patiently.

"You are to take that path," she pointed over the hill to the Copelands', "and tell Joe's mother I will marry and go away if she will give me one of her pictures of Joe."

Her father could only stare at her.

"And if you will not do this, nothing you say or do can make me marry Caleb Evans."

As William Kellogg looked at his daughter—a woman he had never seen before—he knew there was indeed nothing he could say or do.

He took the path to the Copelands'.

"Here is your picture, Naomi," she heard her father say.

She turned from him, stepping nearer the brook. There she took the picture from the envelop, stood looking down at it. Then, "Thank you, Father," she said quietly, and went with him to the house.

"Shall we unite in prayer?" the minister said after the ceremony. He prayed for this new home: "For—for all who may come into it; yes, each and every one. Bless this Christian man! And, kind Heavenly Father, bless this woman. Guide her. Bless this home she leaves behind—this father and mother, sister and little brother—" Naomi was crying now.

They all stood in the dooryard as she drove away with Caleb and the minister. She turned and saw them still standing there. Again she turned, but home was hidden now, though she could still hear the brook.

BOOK TWO

CHAPTER X

BROOK EVANS said good-by to the girls with whom she had left high school and turned into the Santa Clara street which became the road that passed her home. When she was a little girl the street had more quickly become the road. The flat town had widened on all sides. She crossed the railroad-track. She could remember when there was no railroad. Her mother and father had come here by stage. A long time ago that was—1888. Things were modern now. It was 1907. She watched the afternoon train; a long time you could see it, making its way to the mountains it must cross.

Often Brook got a ride home from school, yet she did not mind the three-mile walk. Anyway not now, for it was late May and the valley bright with flowers. You looked across this blowing color to mountains you had to cross to get to Denver and the East. The snow had gone from the lower mountains now, higher and higher would become the snow-line, but Big Chief kept his white crown all through the summer. She liked to stoop for the blue and yellow flowers, and from the fragrant May mildness of the valley lift her eyes to snow.

As she left the town she took a letter from one of her books.

"Dear Brook: Would you go with me to the dance at the Santa Clara Club next Friday evening? Don't refuse me—dear. I am anxiously awaiting your reply.
"Your faithful—and affectionate friend,
"Tony."

The "dear" was smaller and fainter penciling. But the "affectionate" was not faint, as if he had grown bolder. Brook read the note a number of times.

Could she go? She had not gone to dances, for their church did not believe in it. But she had danced at the girls' houses. Her mother knew she danced. Mother would say yes to this, but Father was more strict. And then Tony was Catholic. Even that, her mother would not mind. But her father would. It seemed right her father should feel that way, and a little queer her mother had no such feeling. But perhaps she could "coax him."

She got from her bag the package Mrs. Allen had asked her to bring from the drugstore. Mrs. Allen had the last house at their edge of town. It had been a house in the country; now it was "the outskirts of town." Old Mrs. Allen was good to her. "I helped bring her into the world," she would say. "Oh, how the wind did blow that March night!" She would get Brook a piece of hot bread, or pudding she had saved from dinner.

Now particularly Brook liked stopping, for Mrs. Allen's daughter, Mrs. Waite, was there. She was a missionary home from the Near East, from far places "east of Constantinople." It had a far-away, beautiful sound to Brook. Sylvia Waite was home to raise money for destitute Armenians. She had addressed a large meeting in the town, all the churches united for it. Sometimes it came into Brook's mind that it would be nice to have Mrs. Waite for a mother; that is, she would loyally follow it, it would be nice for some girl who didn't have a mother. Mrs. Waite was beautiful when she told of her homeless children, of how Jesus wanted us to care for all His children. She had such a strong, good smile. She looked right at you as she took your hand and pressed it. In so kind, confident a voice she would say she knew Christian America would not let the least of God's little ones starve. Many had cried when she talked of it. Brook had—and her father looked as if he felt like crying; but her mother had not cried.

"And how is our girl to-day?" Mrs. Waite asked heartily. It was nice to rest in their sitting-room. Mrs. Allen was sad, for they had learned her daughter would not be able to remain as long as they had hoped, but must soon return to those far places east of Constantinople, where her work "called her."

"You will stop often and see Mother," she turned
to Brook. "It is going to be hard to leave her."
There were tears in her eyes as she added, smiling:
"But there is God's work to do." "Yes," the mother
agreed, and it was as if God were with them in the
cheerful sitting-room that looked across the wide
valley to mountains from which the snow did not go.
Brook felt at home with them, and when she left
she felt lifted up, as if she could run and sing, because of God's goodness and His great works
through Mrs. Waite. The exaltation sent her along
with buoyant step, until soon it was as if she were
dancing with Tony.

A new house was going up. Once there had been
no houses between the Allen place and theirs. Her
mother had been alone on the prairie. (Mother
called it the prairie, though others called it the valley. "It is *not* a valley," her mother once cried—
and strange she should be so angry about it.) Perhaps it was because Mother had so long been without neighbors that she did not care for them now.

Brook came in sight of home. It had been very
small, the plainest kind of frame house, but last year
a wing was added, and this made a nice room for
Brook. Her mother had insisted on this room, for
Brook's little upstairs room was close, shut off only
by a pine partition. Now she was much more to
herself. She could look over the valley to Big Chief.

Mother was out working in the flower-bed she had

planted under Brook's window. They had not had many flowers, and their place looked bare. Father had planted a few things, but they had not done well. It was hard, on account of the long dry times. She noticed how her mother stooped, carrying the bucket of water to the flowers beneath Brook's window.

"Hoo-ho!" called Brook. *"Moth-*er!"

"How are you, dear?" There was always anxiety in her mother's voice, and as if—as if she were more glad than she thought she ought to let you know. Mother had looked lonely, carrying the water to the flowers.

"Father not home?"

"No; he's working with the Scotts to-day."

Sometimes Father worked with the Scotts, sometimes they worked with him.

"I stopped at Mrs. Allen's," Brook explained.

Her mother poured a dipper of water on the plants. "Did you?" she asked, a little coldly.

"Mother!" Brook stepped nearer. "Do you suppose Father would let me go to a dance in town next Friday?"

Her mother raised up and looked at her. Brook knew that she was blushing, so she laughed.

"All the girls go. At the Santa Clara Club."

"Who—who would you go with, Brook?"

"Tony. Tony Ross. He asked me."

Again she felt her face flush, as she said his name. Her mother did not speak.

"Do you think Father would let me go?"

"Why wouldn't he let you go?" The answer surprised Brook. It seemed to have surprised her mother, too, it had come so quick and harsh. She turned back to the plants.

"Well, you know how he is," said Brook. "Dancing. You know—it's against his principles."

Carefully, bent low, her mother was pouring water on green things just above the ground.

"And then Tony's a Catholic. Do you think that matters, Mother? What difference can it make, about going to a dance? He—he's nice. He goes to agricultural school. He's Agnes Ross's brother. That's how I met him. They have a big place over on the Monte Vista road.

In the kitchen Brook would look at her mother from time to time, for she had not said yes or no about the dance. Was Mother tired? What was the matter? She would begin to do a thing, then stop, though some things she did twice. "I'll help with supper," Brook volunteered.

"You can rest a little first, dear. It's a long walk for you."

Brook liked her room this hour in the afternoon. She and her mother had painted things nice colors. Mother had done most of it, and Mother had made the bright rag rug. This was the hour the valley became beautiful. The sun was low and there was a light over the valley and the mountains that made it—like heaven, was what Brook thought to say of it.

She would put on her house dress and go out and help. But changing her dress she lingered at the mirror, pulling her hair this way and that. Her hair had a nice wave. When she was a little girl Mother used to brush it round her finger and make curls, for it was soft, you could make it do things. Thick, too, and there was gold in the brown. Her eyes were like that, a brown in which there were gold lights. "Where did you get those brown eyes?" Mrs. Allen would tease. "Your mother's are blue, and your father—he has light eyes." Hands behind her head, she looked in the glass. Her chemise had slipped from one shoulder. One wore a low-neck dress to a dance. She arranged her chemise as if it were a dress to wear in the evening. She knew that her shoulders and her throat were beautiful. Yes, as beautiful as the pictures you saw of people dressed this way.

"Mother," she called, hearing her in the little hall between this room and the rest of the house, "what would I wear—if I went to the dance?"

Her mother stood in the doorway, looking at her. Why, what was the matter? Was Mother going to cry?

"We'll see, dear," was all her mother said, as she turned away.

CHAPTER XI

BROOK was undecided whether to ask her father to-night, or talk with her mother again and get her help. Her instinct was for asking him herself. It was Mother who had asked for the room and there had been a good deal of trouble about that, whereas things Brook asked herself, if they did not involve Father's principles, he was more than likely to do for her. That new coat last winter, though it was true, as he said, he couldn't well afford it; Father didn't seem to have as good luck as those around him, though none worked harder. Mother had become angry when he said the old coat would have to do; afterwards Brook went into the kitchen, where her father sat alone, as often in the evening, his feet on the stove, his head bent, as if thinking. She had sat down near him and said, "The trouble is, Father, all the girls have the new kind of coats. Mine is old-fashioned. I do hate to wear it. It makes me feel different. Of course I know you do everything you can for me. It isn't the way Mother said, and Mother didn't mean those things. I'd just love to have a new coat this winter, so I could look like the other girls." Her father had sat thinking; at last looked up at her. "All right, Brook," he had said.

Her father had let her have the puppy too, though for years, ever since her little brother John was killed, he had refused to have another pup around. Brook was eight when this happened to them. John was not yet five. He had gone running after his puppy. Then a stampede of cattle from the next field. Her mother saw it first, saw them coming. "Caleb! Caleb!" she had screamed, and both of them went running—oh, how fast her father had run! But no—to this day Brook put her hands over her mouth as she saw it. He was trampled—before their eyes. The little boy died in his father's arms as he carried him home.

A silent winter that had been. Father was unable to work. He sat still and looked—horror in his eyes, as if he went on seeing—seeing. Mother had done a good deal of Father's work for him, doing the chores as well as housework, and had taken care of Father, who was like one sick.

Brook, now bringing in kindling for her mother, saw her father returning from the Scotts'. He moved slowly, stiff, as he had for years, ever since he had run so fast, and in vain, that day about ten years ago.

"Hello, Father," she called. "How are you?"

"Guess I'm all right. How's yourself?" Her father had a high voice, sometimes it embarrassed Brook when he spoke in church, though she was ashamed of herself for feeling ashamed. His voice had not slowed with his movements, and that made it seem quicker, higher than it used to be.

"Look at Big Chief," said Brook, for this was a thing in which she and her father shared pleasure, the way the mountains to the east took fire after the sun had set. Mother did not care for it, for she did not like the mountains. This seemed strange to Brook. "They shut me in," her mother said. "But you can get over them," Brook might answer. Her mother would reply, "I will never get over them," and it was true that since Mother came here more than eighteen years before, she had never been over them.

The light which the sun left behind—like a blessing, Brook sometimes thought it, for she often thought things in words of church—came in at their windows as they sat in the kitchen at supper, after Father washed his face and hands at the sink and Mother got things from the stove.

"I had a nice visit with Mrs. Waite," Brook said, especially wanting to be on good terms with her father to-night, and the missionaries was another interest they shared.

"There is a true Christian woman," her father said, after she had told how Mrs. Waite must soon return to those far places east of Constantinople.

"It would be wonderful to be a missionary," Brook agreed.

"Nonsense!" her mother said sharply.

Her father's voice went higher. "Doing God's work—you call that nonsense?"

Brook looked from the window, an instinct to look away when there was this kind of silence between her parents. From her place at table she looked, not toward town, the other way, down where willows grew along the irrigation ditch. Some one was coming on horseback, riding before the willows, that path from the Monte Vista road to theirs. He turned up the road toward the Evans'.

"Well, for goodness' sake," cried Brook, "who is that coming? And why is he coming here?"

Her father glanced out. "What makes you so sure he's coming here?"

But Brook—and her mother—watched the young man riding toward them in the light diffused from Big Chief.

"Well!" cried Brook, as if irritated, and ran to her room to do something to her hair, throw her cape over her house dress. Then she stepped out to examine the plants under her window.

She turned, as if in surprise, when a horse stopped.

"Why, Tony Ross! What are you doing on this road?"

"Oh—maybe I'm just taking a ride," said Tony, in a teasing way his soft voice had, a voice which seemed to be saying more than the words. He leaned toward her, smiling, and his eyes smiling.

"But I didn't know you came home from school this week."

"I made a special trip." He swung from his horse, came over to the flower-bed. "I had a reason."

"You did?" said Brook, as if not concerned with this.

Tony was tall—very straight (they said he had Indian blood. "Indian blood" didn't matter, if it weren't too recent). He moved easily, with grace. He was strong. His eyes were laughing—tender too—when Brook looked up.

"It's a nice night to be riding," she said hastily.

"I think it would be a nicer night to be walking," said Tony, and they laughed together in happy embarrassment.

"I'm going to walk down as far as the willows," Brook went in the house to tell them.

"Who's that you're with?" her father asked.

"Brother of one of her school friends. I know about it," her mother replied hastily.

Tony's horse Major followed. As they turned to speak to him Brook saw her mother sitting on the porch, looking after them. Brook waved, and Mother returned the wave. Tony, too, threw up his hand in salute.

Her father was alone in the kitchen when she returned, head bent as if thinking, the way he so often sat before going to bed.

"Who is this fellow?" he asked.

"Oh, he's Agnes Ross's brother," said Brook, as if it were unimportant. "They have that nice place on the Monte Vista road."

"You could've entertained him here at home, not gone off down there to the willows."

Her mother appeared. "Young folks like to be out on summer nights," she said.

"Yes," said her father. "Yes," he repeated, then added, his voice high with excitement: "The place for a nice girl to entertain her company is in her own front room."

"Goodness!" cried Brook. "What a fuss about walking a few steps down the road!"

She did not at once go to sleep. From her bed she could look out at the stars; she again heard the lapping water in the irrigation ditch, heard the willows which bent over the stream. They had watched the last light from Big Chief, reflected in the water. When they turned they saw the crescent moon. Tony said this was good luck, and put his arm around her. She had moved away, for it didn't seem she should let him do that—not—not yet. But now she lived again each touch, look, word. Slowly they had walked home, part of the way arm in arm; more and more stars came out, a great arch of stars over their wide valley. Tony's eyes had looked down into hers as he held her hands in saying good-night, held them long, close, his eyes looking into hers.

Just as she was getting sleepy a shutter began to bang. Drowsily she lay there hoping it would stop.

"O dear!" she cried at last, springing up in irritation as she knew there was nothing to do but go and fasten it.

She decided it was upstairs, in the little room that used to be hers. As she was starting quietly up, not to wake them, for she could hear Father snoring in the front upstairs bedroom where he and Mother slept, her mother rose from the hallway window at the head of the stairs.

"It's all right," whispered Brook, "just me. Why, Mother," she added, "haven't you been to bed?" For she saw that her mother had not undressed. "Is anything the matter?"

"No; oh, no," her mother answered. "Only—I wasn't sleepy."

"You were sitting here by the window."

"Yes," her mother admitted. "It's such a nice night."

"It is a wonderful night," Brook agreed, talking very low, not to wake her father. "Down there by the water, it was lovely."

"Was it, Brook?" her mother asked, surprising Brook, for the question came so quickly, as if it **were** important.

CHAPTER XII

" I 'D like to have Bess. Brook and I need to go in town this morning."

Brook, still in her room, for Mother let her sleep on Saturday mornings, heard this. Mother hadn't said anything to her about going to town; Mother herself seldom went in. Perhaps it was something about the dance! Had her mother spoken to Father about it last night?

She got up and was dressing while outside there was the kind of talk which always goes on when a horse is asked for on a farm. This was a very bad morning to take Bess—the potatoes. Why hadn't she asked for her day before yesterday? Well, she could have her Monday afternoon. But Mother was firm. She must go in this morning. "I ask for her little enough," she said, when it became necessary to say this. It was so true that, grumbling, her father submitted.

"What are we going to do, Mother?"

"You'll see," her mother replied, almost gayly.

"No, wait a minute," she said, as Brook took the pitcher to pour milk on her oatmeal. "Here—" in

the cupboard she took a cup from behind some jars.
"I saved a little of this for you."

Brook frowned as she poured the cream on her
oatmeal. It was a habit of her mother's thus to
hide the nicest things for her. Sometimes Brook
would protest, "I don't want things that Father
doesn't have." "Well, I don't have them either,"
her mother might say. "Then why should I have
them?" Brook would demand. "Mother loves to
give them to you, darling. Mother can give you so
little." Brook would eat the delicacy saved for her,
though she did not like this habit of her mother's.

"Did you ask Father—about the dance?"

"No, I didn't ask him."

"Oh. I thought maybe we were going in about
that."

"Did you say it was at Carson's they had the
new dress-goods?"

"Mother! Am I going to have a new dress?"

"That might be it, mightn't it?"

Brook jumped up. She wanted to hug her
mother. Why didn't she? She so seldom did anything like that, and her mother would have loved it.
Somehow, it wasn't natural to do it, though she half
knew her mother was starving for it. Perhaps that
was why she couldn't.

Where had Mother got the money? She did not
inquire. Often there was "a little saved up" when

there was something Brook very much wanted.
Sometimes there were quarrels about money. Brook
hated it, for it made it seem they were not nice
people. Mother would say she had to have a new
dress, some things for the house, a woman couldn't
get along with nothing. Then more than likely the
old dress would be made over again, and it was surprising how much there was "put by" when Brook's
new room was to be furnished. One night, coming
in the kitchen after she was supposed to have gone
to bed, she saw her mother going through Father's
pocketbook. She pretended not to have seen, and
she felt uncomfortable about despising her mother
for this, for she knew it was she who profited by it.

As they were tying Bess on a side street, two of
the girls drove up in a runabout. She felt their
buggy looked countrified. It was an old-fashioned
coat her mother was wearing, the only one she had.
In fact, it was made from the coat Brook had dis-
carded. Because she was secretly ashamed of her
mother—her hat, too, all out of style—she introduced her warmly and took her arm as they walked
to the store.

"Oh, the lovely colors!" her mother said, under
her breath, as the clerk unwound the new silk muslins—green, pink, blue, yellow. Carefully her
mother took the yellow one in a hand roughened by
kitchen and farm.

"Maybe the blue one," Brook suggested.

"Whichever one you like." But again she was draping the pale soft yellow.

"You like this one, don't you, Mother?"

"It might be more unusual. And—" she spoke in undertone, for the clerk not to hear, "it would do nice things to your hair and eyes—bring out those lights. With some kind of an ornament, deeper—the color of gold."

Now Brook could see herself that way—golden. Suddenly the blues and pinks were insipid.

"I used to wear pink and blue a good deal," her mother said as they drove home. "But I had blue eyes."

"Well, you still have blue eyes," laughed Brook.

"Have I?" her mother asked.

"Did you used to go to dances—you and Father?"

"Not much," her mother said, and she had turned the other way, looking to the mountains which shut them from the East.

"Guess people didn't dance so much in those days. But then Father never did dance, did he?"

"Not that I know of," said her mother.

"I suppose it was always against his principles."

Her mother did not reply.

"You know," Brook laughed, "I can't imagine Father—going to see a girl—falling in love—proposing. But that's a mean thing to say," she added. "A silly thing to say."

"Oh, I don't know," said her mother, it seemed coldly.

"The valley has colors as beautiful as the muslins," Brook volunteered, after a silence.

"There ought to be trees!" Brook just a little wanted to laugh. Funny her mother should break out like that, as if the valley were a person she had something against. "It's too big and flat. It's too dry," she said excitedly.

"How will we make the dress, Brook?" This time her mother broke the pause. "I'm sorry they didn't have the pattern, but there isn't time to send for it. At the neck I think it would be nice—simple. The way you had your chemise pulled down yesterday."

"But we've bought the dress—and I haven't asked Father yet."

"Never mind," her mother said. "I say you can go to the dance."

This seemed strange. Brook was a little troubled.

CHAPTER XIII

"NO; I'll stay home and have dinner all ready when you get back," her mother said about going to church.

Father did not like this. A family should go together to God's house, he held. But Mother often said she was tired or had a headache on Sunday morning.

Going to church was important to Father. Brook could not remember when he had missed, except at times the winter storms made it impossible to cross the valley. Rain, no ordinary bad weather, kept him at home. Even that winter—"that winter" meant the one after her little brother was killed—Father had gone. Mother had gone with him then; indeed she would have to get him ready to go. She would bring the hair brush. "Now the shoes," she would say, for he would forget what there was to do next.

Even now it took Father a long time to get ready for church. He took his bath the night before, but Sunday morning he shaved, trimmed his beard. Now he was out on the back porch, brushing his coat, his shoes. You could not hurry him, though even so he would not be late, for he began early. In his Sunday shoes, which squeaked, you realized how slowly he moved about the house.

Brook waited in her room, all ready in her dark blue suit, the white waist with the pleated collar, which Mother had ironed the afternoon before. It was her nicest thin waist, so Mother was always doing it up for her. There were rosebuds on her hat, and she wore her gray gloves, which she had cleaned. She carried her little red purse, her own contribution to the collection.

Mother came in with a tape-measure. "Oh, you look nice, dear," she said. "Unbutton your jacket, will you? I want to get your measure."

Brook knew that when they were gone Mother would work on the dress, though Father did not approve of sewing on Sunday.

"Do you think I should say something—on the way to church?"

"No, not on Sunday. Anyway," her mother added, with irritation, "didn't I tell you I was going to manage it?"

This seemed uncertain, dangerous, to Brook, particularly after what happened the night before. Tony had ridden over again, for his answer about the dance. She asked him in this time, though they couldn't talk so well, embarrassed in the stiff front room. She had gone out and asked her mother to come in and meet Tony, for this seemed proper to Brook; it was what nice people did in stories. And Mother had acted like nice people, even though she was in her house dress. She was quiet, but her face had something that made you know, as you did at times, that Mother had been pretty when she was a girl. Her voice was nice—Mother did have a beautiful voice. It was too bad she had had to work so hard, and been so much by herself. She had stayed with them a little while—not too long, and yet not as if she felt she should hurry away. After Mother had been there it was easier to talk than when they were alone in the beginning.

Brook stepped outdoors when Tony was leaving. They petted his horse. Perhaps it was a long time they had been out there when a window opened upstairs and her father called: "Time to come in now, Brook." She and Tony had laughed about it, they really didn't mind; but Mother had been angry. "Oh, I am sorry, dear," she said, and Brook heard her saying sharp things after she went upstairs.

As she and her father held the hymn-book together, standing while they sang, Brook's thoughts were mixed. "I am so glad that Jesus loves me." Brook's gladness was because of both Jesus and Tony. Brook really liked going to church; it made her feel lifted up, and even when she was bored, when the minister preached too long, she had a sense of being part of things as they should be, of being taken in where she was one with others.

Mrs. Allen and Mrs. Waite were across the aisle, a little in front of them. It was nice to watch Mrs. Waite, standing erect, as if indeed glad Jesus loved her, confident. Her clothes were good style. Missionaries did not need to be dowdy, as most of them were, in their pictures. Watching her standing there so strong, sure, happy, Brook thrilled to think of how she would return to far places east of Constantinople, where she gave her life to all the little ones who needed her. Mrs. Waite was really older than her mother; she looked years younger, as if God had blessed her for her good works. Brook, too, felt blessed, just to be standing near her and singing the same song.

At first she listened to the sermon, about John, the beloved disciple, but soon she and the sermon were separated, and she was out there in the night with Tony; now, even more than at the time, there was something exciting in their low tones, though for the most part it was of usual enough things they talked. Through the whole latter half of the sermon Brook was standing there with Tony, beside his horse—standing closer and closer to him as the sermon she did not hear sent her farther into a voluptuous drowse.

It was only about a month ago she had first talked with Tony. For some time she had occasionally seen him in town, and always he had seemed "different," perhaps it was the Indian blood; then, too, his father was a foreigner. He came into town in an automobile, wearing clothes better, less sober, than the young men of Santa Clara. His skin was rather dark, and his dark eyes quick-moving, laughing; Brook knew that he thought about her; when they passed he would look at her as though he were saying something to her. But Brook did not speak to young men she had not met.

Then one Saturday afternoon Madge Atkins had a birthday party and Tony called for his sister. Agnes introduced him, and as Tony shook hands with Brook and said, "Pleased to meet you, Miss Evans," his eyes were laughing, as if he had been meeting her all along. "Well, if we're going, we're going," Agnes said several times; but Tony lingered, talking to Brook. Last night he had said, in a voice low, caressing: "Brook—Brook—why are you named Brook?" "Because Mother loved the brook she heard when she was a girl." "Your mother named you for a brook she used to know?" She saw how much the idea pleased him. "Your mother loved the brook, and I—I love Brook." Many times, after she had gone to bed, and again now, she dwelt with the words, each shade of the voice, until it was a part of her, as were his eyes, looking down into hers, leaning from his horse as he said good-night.

"Praise God from whom all blessings flow!" sang Brook, holding the hymn-book with her father, and looking buoyantly over at Mrs. Waite, who sang buoyantly.

Many wanted to shake hands with the returned missionary, but she saw Brook and came to her. "And how is our girl this morning?" "Our girl" she always said, joining her mother's claim. She was pleasant with Father, too. "And how do you *do* this morning, Brother Evans?" she asked, in a happy voice, and as if it really mattered to her. Father liked it, and even tried to joke, to be gallant. "Not feelin' so bad right this minute," he said, shaking her hand. Mrs. Waite laughed in a way that made him feel good, and he greeted the others with more spirit than was usual with him.

"Mother not feeling well?" Mrs. Allen asked, always kindly about Mother, though Brook felt something of disapproval behind it. "Mother gets tired," Brook said.

She and Father talked about church affairs as they drove home. They were used to the ride together, and were without constraint when not talking. They would say the valley was in good shape, or that it needed rain, and then there could be a silence without awkwardness. Brook, leaning to one side, looking over the valley, was thinking of Tony, and it seemed quite right and natural she should be driving home from church with her father, thinking things which of course she would not say. That was a state of affairs in which she felt at home.

Brook said Mrs. Waite was "lovely." "There is a true Christian woman," he said, as always of her. After that pause he added: "It's better to have most of your friends inside your own church. You know who people are then, and you all have the same way of looking at things." This of course meant Tony. Brook smiled as she thought of the young men of their church, compared with Tony.

Mother was hurrying, as if behind; no, dinner was not quite ready. When she went to her room, on the bed Brook saw a yellow ruffle under a towel which did not entirely cover it. Mother had been in here working on the dress. Oh, she had done lovely things! When she took off her church clothes Brook held the dress up to her. She had never looked like this. She was beautiful! Happily singing: "Holy, Holy, Holy, Lord God Almighty!" she went out to help with dinner.

CHAPTER XIV

LOOKING back to it afterwards—long afterwards—it seemed to Brook the nicest times she and her mother ever had together were in making the dress she was to wear to the dance. There was a good deal of work, for they were doing it by hand, and some stitching—embroidery, indeed, in a deeper yellow, the color of gold. They worked in Brook's room, usually after Father had gone to bed—"No use having it around," her mother said. Brook even talked about Tony. Didn't her mother think he was handsome? Didn't he have a nice voice? He was—oh, different, somehow. He would be through school now in a few weeks. What was he going to do, her mother asked. Brook told about Tony's uncle in California. He had a vineyard, and olive-trees. He wanted Tony to come out and go in with him. Tony thought he would do that, it was a good chance. "And he said—he said to me"—Brook couldn't keep from telling this, though she knew she was blushing, and told it as a joke—" 'Do you think you would like California, Brook?' Now why should he think—"

She had not finished it, for her mother's hands closed over her sewing.

"Oh, Mother," Brook cried, because of the eyes that looked at her, "don't worry. I haven't gone yet!"

"Do you think you would like California?" her mother asked, quietly, after they had stitched more gold thread into the pale yellow dress. Her mother did not raise her eyes from her work as she asked this question.

"Well," said Brook, "well, I don't know—yet."

Wind shook the house. They did not talk much more that night.

It was the night before her mother had told more about herself as a girl than she had ever told. "The brook ran between big trees. I heard it from my room. There were wonderful smells from the fields all around. That is rich country. When you spade into the earth it is black and rich—not desert like this. In the nights—the wind in the trees—back home the wind is not unfriendly, like this, but beautiful, like a great organ."

"And you had good times at home, Mother?"

"Yes."

"Mother—do you mind telling me—did you—did you have any other beaus, before you married Father?"

At first it seemed Mother did mind telling. Then, "Yes, Brook," her mother had answered.

It seemed too bad Mother had never been back
home. She must have been homesick, loving it like
this. She remembered so much, even about the dog.
Patsy was his name. Father had twice gone to
Illinois. The first time when Brook was a little girl
—something about borrowing money. Then just
three years ago he had to go back; his father died
and things were to be sold. She and her mother
had expected to go with him that time. At the last
minute, "I can't!" she heard her mother say. Brook
was disappointed, and cross about it. She had not
been nice to her mother while they were there alone.

"Will we go back there some day?" Brook asked
now. "And hear the brook?"

"I hope that some day you and I will go back
there together—and hear the brook."

Mother's voice—it was low, but steady, strong—
as if something were behind it. The words, the way
they were spoken, made Brook look at her mother.
She wore a plain calico house dress—the kind she always wore; her hair was brushed straight back. She
was thin, and stooped. Her face, too, was thin,
but if Mother would "take a little pains with herself"—something in her eyes, about her mouth . . .
She did not look like people around her. Often
Brook wished her mother did look more like the
other girls' mothers. But sometimes, as now, she
had a kind of—was it beauty? A—meaning?
What would you call it?

Mother's mother and father had both died. Her father only the year before. "Wouldn't you like to go?" Brook's father asked, when they got the letter saying Grandfather Kellogg could live only a few days. Mother had thought about it, then said, No. But she scarcely spoke through those days.

Now her brother, Brook's Uncle Willie, whom she had never seen, had the old place, with his wife and children. Mother's sister Rosie lived in the town. Sometimes they heard from her. Not often. Sewing together Mother told stories about her young sister Rosie, and her little brother Willie.

It was Wednesday evening the trouble began. The dress was finished, and Brook had tried it on. Oh, it was lovely! She was excited, and Mother was excited too. It had grown cool in Brook's room, so they went to the kitchen. They had forgotten about being quiet, not to wake Father. They heard him coming down the stairs!

Mother had the lamp on the floor, for she was rearranging the hem. "Go into your room," she whispered; but by the time the lamp was out of the way Father had opened the door.

He carried his bed-lamp. He was wearing his long nightshirt.

"What's going on down—" he began crossly. Then he saw Brook, stood staring at her.

"How do you like my new dress, Father?" she asked.

"What's that for?"

"A school party," her mother answered. "The school boys and girls," she added, as Brook looked at her.

The dress had almost no sleeves. The neck was low, as Brook had wanted it.

"You're not going to wear it like that?" he demanded.

"It is an evening dress," said Brook.

Her father turned to her mother. "You make that dress decent or she'll not set foot from this house in it!"

To Brook's astonishment her mother was saying, "Oh, very well; if you insist I'll put in a yoke, with sleeves."

"Yes!" he cried. "I do insist!" And Brook was afraid for the lamp, his hand moved so violently. "I do insist," he repeated, as he turned to the stairs.

"Now it's all spoiled!" stormed Brook. "What will it *look* like? A yoke—and sleeves!"

"Don't, dear. Never mind. Don't you see? I'll make it as a separate waist," said her mother softly. "You can show it to him that way, and then—take it out."

Brook could scarcely believe this was what she heard. She had several feelings at once: a kind of admiration—she herself would not have thought of this, at least not so quickly; relief—and disapproval. If *she* had thought of it—but it seemed a queer thing for a mother to be proposing to a daughter.

They heard him coming back down the stairs.

"S-h!" her mother warned. "Don't say much. I will—"

"What kind of a party is this?" he demanded.

"A dancing party," said Brook.

"Dancing party? I thought you were a Believer?"

"All the girls dance now," her mother said.

"Because other people do wrong—that any *reason* for doing wrong?"

"I don't think it is wrong, Father," said Brook. "It's true that times have changed."

She said it reasonably, and he was calmer. But suddenly he asked: "Who is it you're going with?"

"Tony," said Brook.

"This young fellow that comes around here? We don't know nothing about him."

"Oh, I know a good deal about him," replied Brook. "His sister is a friend of mine. I know he's of a nice family, and he's a gentleman."

"I'll find out about that!" said her father.

"What have you to do with it?"

Brook turned to her mother, unable to believe those were the words she heard. It was a strange silence the words left between her mother and father. He held his lamp in a hand which shook. Neither of them spoke until, "Go to bed, Brook," her mother said.

CHAPTER XV

HER father was in the field when Brook got up the next morning. She was cross, for it seemed to her now her mother had spoiled everything. This was Thursday; to-morrow night was the dance; and after the way things had gone last night—the way her father had stood there looking at her mother when she said, "What have you to do with it?"—(*what* a question!) now the chances of her "getting around him" as she might have done in the first place—oh, it was all spoiled! Mother got her the dress, but what was there to do with it? She petulantly pushed aside the cream her mother had saved for her. Mother even was so silly as to say, "Don't worry, dear."

"Don't worry!" she repeated tempestuously, starting for school.

Her father was in town. At noon she saw him coming out of the bank. She took pains he should not see her, for she was "mad at him"; yet she was more resentful toward her mother, who had managed it so badly, spoiling everything.

The girls talked of nothing but the dance, and Brook pretended she was going. This finally gave

her the feeling she was going, and through the afternoon study hour she sat thinking of things she could
say to her father.

It was he who spoke of it after, almost in silence,
they finished supper that night.

"Guess you don't set much store by this young
man, do you, Brook?"

"What young man?" Brook asked coldly.

"Oh, guess you know. This Tony Rossi."

"Are you talking about Tony Ross?" laughed
Brook.

"His name is Rossi—Italian."

"Guess I ought to know what his name is! I've
known his sister for more than a year!"

"Oh, they keep names pretty straight at the
bank," observed her father. "They did change it
to Ross. Wanted to be American."

"Anything wrong in being American? I don't
thank you for running to the bank to look up my
friends! I'm eighteen years old!"

"Well, you wouldn't be the first girl of eighteen
—or nineteen either—needed to be looked after
and kept safe."

Even in her anger Brook was aware of the low
sound from her mother, so strange a sound.

"Kept *safe*," scoffed Brook. "You talk as if—
What's the matter with Tony—if his name was Italian? I knew his father was a foreigner. What's
the difference?"

"First place, he's a Catholic."

"Well, I'm not so narrow-minded I think all my friends have to belong to my church."

"You couldn't marry a Catholic."

"Who said anything about marrying?"

"It's not right a young girl go round with a man she can't marry."

Her mother was sitting behind Brook, but facing her father. He did not look at her mother, even when there was now the sound of a moving chair.

"More than that, he's a half-breed."

"You mean his Indian blood?" laughed Brook. "Indian blood—a long way back?"

"Not such a long way. I made it my business to find out about them. His grandfather was an Easterner, come out here in the first day and got land. The first wife died, and he took up with a squaw—this young man has a squaw grandmother —that's the Indian blood. Their child—daughter of this settler and the squaw, married the young man's father—Antone Rossi. And do you know what he was? He was an Italian laborer."

"I guess we're all laborers, aren't we?" parried Brook, her face burning, for she didn't like the sound of it, put this way. "They have a lots better house than we have! Have we an automobile? They dress better than we do—I can tell you that!"

"And where did they get their money to dress better than we do? I'll tell you where, if you don't know. The Dago started a saloon, money he got from the half-breed wife. That was over other side of the range. There's plenty of poor fools willing to give for drink what they should give to their families and the Lord. Well, after they'd made enough they moved over here, took land, educated their children—"

"I should think they did," cried Brook. "Sent them to college!"

"Yes, all right, college. Maybe in time they can live down their past. I hope so. But guess you can see for yourself, if you think it over, this mess isn't anything for you to get mixed up with."

For the moment Brook had no reply. Her father added: "What do you think Sister Waite would say?"

Suddenly her mother was between her and her father, standing there behind the table, hands resting heavily on it, leaning forward. She had never seen her mother like this. Deep red burned in her cheeks, and her eyes were like something hard and bright. It made Brook almost afraid. "Sister Waite! Sister Waite! You and the missionaries are to say what my daughter is to do?"

Her father looked at her mother, and then he looked down, turning a little away. Brook had a feeling she should defend her father, should be saying, "Of course Father has something to say about what I shall do," but that would be going over to his side. She wanted, in spite of everything, to get to the dance.

Her mother spoke more quietly. "This is not a question of marrying. It is going to a party. These young people—this young man and his sister—stand well in the town. They belong to the nicest crowd there is here. Brook does not lower herself in going with him. Brook, I say you may go to the dance."

How her mother was trembling!

Her father got up, facing her mother. His head moved back and forth, as if something had happened at the back of his neck. "I have got something to say about it!" His voice was higher than ever, and shook as his head shook. "Deny that if you can! I know my Christian duty, and what I say is *No*. You hear me? No! As this is my house and God is my Judge, I say No!" It was not to her, it was to her mother he kept saying No.

As she saw them like this, frightened, Brook cried: "Oh, such a *fuss*—about a little fun! Other girls don't have all this trouble about—about—" She was sobbing and her mother moved toward her, but Brook stepped back. "I'll just stay here at home then! Forever! I might as well be *old*. I might as well be *dead*. I wish I was—I wish—" Unable to stop now: "What was I born at all for!" Brook cried in a loud voice, and then, face covered, sobbing wildly, she went from the room, leaving them there together—silent now.

CHAPTER XVI

IN school the next day Brook composed notes, one of which she would give Agnes Ross for Tony. *"Dear Tony: I cannot tell you how sorry I am, but I am unable to go to the dance. My father, I fear, is a little old-fashioned."* No, that was ridiculous. *"Will you forgive me, and for not letting you know sooner, but I didn't know myself until last night that it is not possible—"* No. *"Dear Tony, I cannot go to the dance. My father won't let me. He doesn't believe in dancing. I am broken-hearted—"* No, not broken-hearted, and so each note was either too strong, too unconcerned, too simple or too involved. It ended with her giving no note to Agnes, though she was miserable about this, just making it worse, not letting him know.

Through her disappointment ran faintly an un-reasoned hope. There were moments of seeing her-self in the yellow and gold dress, dancing with Tony, moments of seeing this miserable time behind her. Things did usually come out better than you thought they were going to. Perhaps her mother would do something. She had been shocked by her mother's manner of speaking to her father, and yet she depended on her, willing to take advantage of what she condemned.

Her mother's manner this morning had not given much hope. It was a strange woman moved silently about the house, a woman to make one a little afraid. Brook did not ask any questions. What was the use? Her mother might say Yes, but she knew what her father had said.

Mother had followed her as she was leaving. "Brook!"

"Well?"

"It will all come out right." Brook waited, but her mother added, "If not now—soon. Don't be unhappy, darling!"

Freshly disappointed, "Much use saying that," Brook had cried, as she left her mother alone, alone there on "the prairie" for the day. She had wanted to turn and wave, had almost done so, knowing her mother stood looking after her, but she was so disappointed she had to hurt. More than once through this day she saw her mother standing there waiting for her to look back and wave, saw her then turn to the house.

Her feeling of shock that Tony's father had been an Italian saloon-keeper, that his mother was a half-breed, abated as she saw Agnes Ross among the other girls. Agnes was a gentle girl, soft-voiced— "a lady." She was one of the best-dressed girls in

school. She was going to the party to-night with
Ray Lewis, whose father was president of the bank,
who lent money to Brook's father, to all the people
around there. Yes—the bank! Much they cared—
if there had once been an *i* on the name! After all,
you didn't stay what your people were. No, it was
what you were yourself that counted—why, that
was the very foundation of America, thought
Brook. Her father's, "What would Sister Waite
say?" presented itself, but this conflict within her—
the world against her, a part of her own self against
her, only made the memory of Tony's arm around
her, his eyes looking into hers, his nearness, a more
secret and a more dangerous sweetness. In school
to-day she had thoughts such as she had never had,
as dreaming over her books she was dancing with
him—the long ride home after they had been dancing together.

If she could not go—she hadn't given up—she
would put on her dress, as if she had been intending
to go; she would cry, "O Tony, I am so unhappy—
take me away!" Of course she would say nothing
of the kind, a cooler part of her knew. But she
would cry a little, her eyes would be "swimming in
tears," and he would whisper with a new tenderness:
"Soon it will be different—darling," and before she
could stop him he would fold her in his arms, kiss
her, would not let her go. Then she would be his
—forever.

Mother was upstairs when she got home, and called down, her voice just as loving as if Brook had turned and waved to her: "That you, Brook? How are you, dearie?"

When Brook opened the door of her room she stood gazing at the bed. The new dress had been pressed, and was spread there as if ready to put on. Her underthings, her stockings, her slippers!

"Why, Mother!" she hurried upstairs. "What are my things laid out for?"

"Isn't this the night of the dance?"

"But Father—"

"Father isn't home. Mr. Scott came for him to go down to South Ridge, help with cattle that are sick. He can't be home till ten o'clock to-night."

She was going! She was going to the dance!

Then the rest of it came back. "But Father said I couldn't go."

"Oh, but I said you could."

Brook stood there, doubtful; indeed, disapproving. She herself might defy her father, deceive him, girls did that at times—then were sorry for it, of course; but for her mother to do it for her, in this matter-of-course way, this was a state of things in which she did not know how to move.

"But what will he say—afterwards?"

"Never mind. I will take the responsibility. Listen, dear," as Brook was about to speak, "this is a thing I know more about than your father does.

He—he's queer about things like this, but I'm not going to let him spoil your good times."

Why was Brook not more grateful to her mother? She herself wondered why. Oh, she would go, all right, and yet she was on Father's side. It wasn't right to deceive him like that. Well, she would never do it again. She would tell Tony tonight her father didn't approve of dancing. Of course she had to go now—on account of not having let him know sooner. The reason she hadn't, she now assured herself, was that she had hoped her father would relent. He wasn't home to relent, so she would have to go ahead on her mother's say-so.

Within five minutes she was all excitement about the dance, singing as she took her bath, dancing about the house. Mother was excited too. They had a good time together, getting her ready.

"Coming home," her mother said, "you had better be just as quiet as you can. It might be as well if you stopped over at the north line—and walked in. You can tell Tony that your father is very strict about your being out late—that he hadn't realized how late the party would be."

"O dear!" Brook expostulated.

"Now never mind, dear, don't let it spoil your evening. Lots of girls' fathers are strict, and it's their mothers who understand—and help them. Oh, you are *lovely*, darling!" Her mother stood off and looked at her. There were tears on her mother's face as she murmured, "Brook! Our little girl!"

Brook was embarrassed, but too excited to mind. "I do look nice? I really do, don't I, Mother?" She turned this way and that. Then she did say: "I never would have had the dress but for you, Mother." She did what she was rarely able to do. She put her arms around her mother. "You do everything for me. You are—so good to me."

For one moment her mother leaned her face against her. She was crying, but very quietly. "If only I could give you—everything in the world!"

Theirs was not an automobile road, so Tony was driving out for her. She heard the horse coming!

"O—h!" Tony murmured when he saw her. He held her hands, she had impulsively held out both hands to him, stood looking at her, again said, "O—h!" until she laughed. He seemed able to say very little. He did not take his eyes from her; even when Mother was there it was as if he could not look away from Brook.

Mother stood in the doorway as they drove away in the moonlight.

"Good-by, Mother dear!" Brook called back.

"I'll take good care of her, Mrs. Evans," Tony called; and they laughed, for they were excited, they were happy.

CHAPTER XVII

"OH, I'll have to be quiet. Father's fussy about my being out late." She had forgotten to say it at the north line. They were returning as slowly as the horse would let them, Tony driving with one hand, the other arm around Brook, and her head against his shoulder. It had been the happiest evening she had known in her life. She had felt Tony excited with pride in her at the dance; even among all the other pretty dresses, she had startled as beautiful. Now she knew she was a good dancer—she had not been sure. Tony had to fight for his own dances, but he had insisted, and much of the time they danced together. Radiant with triumphs which were new to her, with a being in love which was new to her, when finally she went to the dressing-room for her things it was a Brook Evans she had never seen before looked at her from the glass. That new Brook Evans excited her as much as all the rest of it had excited; it was as if she saw herself touched into life. The slow ride home together across the fragrant valley— wideness of the still night—the stars so far away—

Tony here so close—yes, she was in love, and it was more than any dream of it!

In low voice they laughed about her father being "fussy"; Tony walked with her to the side door, from which she could most quietly reach her room. "Good-night," she whispered—but there were a number of good-nights, and then, "Oh, Brook— Brook—my darling!" and "Tony!"—a kiss, not timid, as those few kisses when driving home slowly, under the stars.

Major objected to the long wait. He whinnied, stamped, started to turn round and Tony had to call, "Whoa!"

"Quick, and—oh, quiet as you can!" whispered Brook, alarmed now and quickly getting in the house and to her room.

But the horse had the buggy in a position that made necessary backing, turning. Major was nervous, and Tony had to speak to him. It seemed a loud noise when they trotted off, and to her dismay she heard the window go up, her father's, "What's that? Who's there?"

Her mother's voice, trying to quiet him, to make him think it nothing. But he was suspecting!—his voice quick, higher, angry, not heeding her mother.

He was coming downstairs!

Brook had thrown off her coat, wanting to get the dress off at once, to avoid possible trouble. But there had not yet been time—and he coming straight to her room! With one sound, more a thump at the door than a knock, "Brook!" he called, and opened the door. On the bureau was the lamp her mother had left burning low for her.

He was speechless as he looked at her, and in her nervousness she half wanted to laugh—in his nightclothes, mouth open, his beard trembling as he stared; she knew she was flushed, hair disordered, home from the dance to which he had said she could not go, wearing the dress he had forbidden.

"I am sorry I disturbed you, Father."

"Oh!" he cried. "Sorry you *disturbed* me!"

"You weren't home to—talk it over again. I couldn't believe you really meant—"

He seized her arm. "You couldn't—huh? Well, maybe I better show you what I mean!" He had both her arms and was shaking her. "Shall I show you what I mean? You ought to be *whipped*. By God, I'll do it! I'll keep *this* house clean if I have to—"

Her mother was upon him. "Take your hands off my daughter!" She struck his wrists. He let go of Brook.

"Get out of her room!" The low voice was violent. It seemed she was going to strike him. For a moment it was as if anything could happen.

"You want her to go the way you went, do you?"

"I'm not going to have her live the way I've lived!"

Brook did not understand. Something more than just this seemed to be going on between them. It frightened her.

"You and I can talk about that by ourselves," her mother said, a little more naturally. "It's time Brook went to bed."

"I should think it was!" He looked at the clock on Brook's dresser. "Half-past two! Out alone with a low fellow—"

"He's not!" Brook cried.

"Buggy riding with him—after a dance—till half-past two in the morning!" He turned on her mother. "Don't you *want* your daughter to be decent?"

Brook, glad of a grievance that would turn the balance, cried: "You can't say I'm not decent! You can't—"

"Look here, Brook. I'm your father. Isn't that true?"

"Of course," said Brook, sullenly.

"And this is my house. Is that true?"

"Yours and Mother's."

"And yours," he added, changing. "But I'm master in my own house. And I say you cannot go to dances. I say you cannot keep company with this fellow. You heard me, did you?"

"I heard you!"

"They're plain words, aren't they?"

"Plain enough."

"And you know I mean them, don't you?"

Brook threw out her hands. "Stop *talking!*"

"Now I'll let you go to bed," he said, almost gently.

He went up the stairs and closed the door of his room.

Brook, elbows on her dresser, face in her hands, though sobbing with fatigue and anger, knew that her mother had not left the room. As her mother did not speak, curious, Brook looked up.

Her mother's face checked her tears. As their eyes met her mother stepped to the door and closed it. She stood leaning against it.

"Brook!"

"Well?"

"You do not have to obey him."

"Why don't I have to?" Brook asked crossly. "He's my father."

"No," her mother was saying to her. "He is not your father."

CHAPTER XVIII

AT first she thought her mother had gone crazy. Or was it herself, after too much excitement, was hearing things that weren't being said?

"Now I will tell you! Now I will tell you the truth!" But the truth was what it did not seem to be.

Her mother left her and came back with something in her hand. She held this out to Brook. "That is your father."

Brook looked down at a faded photograph. This her father? Why, he was not any older than Tony. And her father had just been in here, in his night-clothes, saying she could not go to dances, forbidding her to keep company with Tony. What a funny-looking collar. And what a way to brush his hair! All dressed-up to have his picture taken—nobody wore a tie like that, and you could see he thought he was very good-looking. "Fresh"—that was it, not at all as a father should look.

"You see, dear?" her mother asked. "Oh, it is fading. It has faded. But you see how beautiful he is—my Joe? His eyes—they have not faded. And his smile? Darling, do you see your father's smile?"

Brook could not look at her mother—her face working like this, one of the teeth gone, almost as if she had become silly, talking about this person, "Joe"—looking like this and talking about eyes, smile.

So Mother had "gone wrong." *Mother*. She was telling about it, as they sat across the table from one another, between them a faded photograph of a fellow wearing funny-looking clothes.

"You look like him, dear. Don't you see it?"

No, Brook did not see it. Well, maybe. It was hard to tell—brown spots of a fading photograph, and such a way of slicking down the parted hair!

It didn't seem nice to be talking about it, Father right here in the house. Tony must be almost home now. Was he thinking about her? Would he be thinking of her—after he had gone to bed?

"They would not let us keep company, but we loved each other so much we could not be separated. The brook ran past his house and past mine. We met by the brook. That was—that was where we were lovers. That is why you are named Brook. I have always wanted to tell you. I did not want you to think this man was your father. He was alive —your own father—strong and handsome and full of life. He was a lover, your father. In his voice —his eyes— Oh, it is beautiful back there at home —in the great summer nights, it is beautiful!"

Brook felt embarrassed. It was as if Mother had taken off too many of her clothes. Father, asleep there upstairs—in that was naturalness, safety. Brook was a little cold in the thin dress she had worn to the dance. For once her mother was not thinking of her that way. Mother had a gray bathrobe over her cotton-flannel nightgown, her hair, turning gray, was brushed straight back and braided for the night. It was a little dreadful—almost foolish—looking as she did, to sit here, way past the middle of the night, talking about love. Tony must be asleep now. Brook's feet ached; she was not used to dancing so long. She thought of herself over there in her bed, warm under the covers. Later she would like to hear this story—killed by the haying machine; it thrilled her that she should be part of a tragic romance. Of course she had always known, she told herself now, there was something about her—different. She was both dazzled and frightened. So this was what could happen! Of course not to her. But Father was right in being afraid —yes, it was right a father should be strict.

"Why, Mother—how terrible for you!" she would keep saying, as her mother told of finding out for herself what no one else knew, told of marrying a man she did not love in order to give a name and a home to her child.

And all the time Brook felt as if this were something that could not be true. In the morning it would not be true.

"I was lying on the bed. I was reading a magazine—about Italy. Italy is a land of love—the orange groves, the olive-trees, the vineyards. For centuries they have been lovers, the Italians. Venice. The murmuring of waters, and the whisperings. And the brook murmuring for me, and Joe's words the night before—'Good-night, darling Naomi.' Then my father—running." Her mother sat straight, her eyes looking right ahead. "His low voice—excited, frightened. I stood in the dining-room and saw them in the kitchen. 'I mean—'" her mother's voice only whispered it—"' 'I mean, he's dead, daughter.'" It seemed her mother was going to fall forward, as if this were something she had learned only now. She reached for the picture. "Joe!" Tears ran down her thin face.

"It was by the brook I first knew about you."

Brook wondered—how she knew. Thoughts like that broke into the current of what she felt she should be feeling.

"My father said, 'Caleb will marry you.'"

"He—knew?" Brook asked.

"Why, of course he knew," said her mother, a little impatiently. "He had asked me before, and of course I refused him. Now he was told, and now—I had to marry him."

"He knew—you were going to have another

man's child?" She felt dramatic, unreal, saying the words.

"And married you, and never let any one know? And never—" It stopped her, for suddenly it had become real, a part of her. Something big was right there. "And never let *me*—" The tears she had felt she should be shedding before, she could not now hold back. One time she remembered above all others. After his little boy, his own son, his only child, had been trampled before his eyes—after the first days of sitting there without speaking (she remembered it, for she had thought he was never going to speak again)—"Well, good-night, Brook," he had said, as she was going to bed. She came nearer and stood before him, both sorrowful and curious. He raised his eyes and looked at her, though he had only looked straight ahead, or down. Fear of him there had been too, he was so strange; so she remembered the look which now at last she understood. He was glad she was there! Not then, nor at any time in all her life, had look or word of his hinted, "You are not my child." With the deepest feeling of her eighteen years Brook Evans whispered, "Father!" and turned from the faded photograph her mother offered.

BOOK THREE

CHAPTER XIX

NAOMI KELLOGG, scrubbing the kitchen floor, moved her pail, looked up and through the open door saw Joe Copeland's daughter looking at Caleb Evans. He had not gone to the field as usual that morning, tired from the late return the day before, and the disturbed night; now he was working about the barnyard, making a fresh place for the little chickens. Brook, sitting on the steps, peeling apples for the Sunday pie, had stopped her work and was looking at the man who fastened chicken wire to the shed.

He worked slowly; his movements were the movements of an old man. Well, he was that— twelve years older than Naomi, and she thirty-eight. Though when had he not been old? But Brook was not looking as at an old man who had never known youth. There was tenderness in the young eyes that regarded Caleb Evans, a tenderness Naomi had never seen there for herself.

He began moving the chicks. "I'll help you, Father," Brook cried.

Not having risen from her knees, Naomi watched them working together, saw Brook hold the yellow, downy little things against her breast, cupped by her hands. Laughingly she looked up at her father as she said, "They're sweet, aren't they? So soft and little!" Just so she had held Brook against her breast, so soft and little.

She finished the floor without again looking, though Brook's laughter and Caleb's high voice came in to her. At the table she saw that the orange she had given her Brook had not eaten. They were a luxury Brook loved; the day they were in town getting the dress she had bought a few, and saved them as surprises. She loved doing this, the thought of having an offering would make Naomi happy, make her feel younger, almost joyous. Even when Brook received it ungraciously, saying, "I don't want things Father doesn't have," she had a satisfaction in seeing her eat the morsel against which she protested. Holding the rejected orange, Brook's laughter and Caleb's voice coming in to her, Naomi Kellogg was frightened as she had not been afraid since those days when she knew that Joe was dead and his child lived.

From that time until last night there had been a thing for which she lived. She would one day tell Brook she was the child, not of a loveless marriage, but of a love nothing had been able to stay. She would give Brook to love, and that would be giving Joe his child. How could you live for a thing nineteen years, then do it as she had done it last night? She raised her eyes to the glass over the sink. She flushed at thought of herself, looking like this, talking of love. But, oh—she had had it! Even yet, she did know it! Where were the words that should have given life to summer nights now deep under other summers?

She went to put away Joe's picture, which she had not returned to the trunk the night before. She held it, thinking what she had paid to get it. If she could have the picture, she had told her father, she would marry Caleb Evans. She looked at it, trying to see how it must look to Brook. It had discolored, as if—as if it had indeed been long dead. Joe dressed better than any of the other boys, but young men dressed differently now. He must have looked very long ago, old-fashioned, perhaps even a little (the word hurt) comical to Brook. She had never thought of that, of how change—change, which she could not control—was against her. They lived in the Now—the young. And the face she had just seen in the glass . . . When she looked at this picture she had always been Naomi. But both Joe and Naomi had been gone a long time.

She put Joe's picture away, deeper in the trunk than it had been. She had thought it would one day be for Brook, the dearest thing she could leave her.

Caleb was moving about down in the kitchen. He put something on the table, in his slow way walked to the sink. Outside Brook was singing. In spite of the shock of the new things she had come to know, she sang because she was young, and Tony loved her. The boy did love her. That was in his eyes as, unable to say a word, he had stood gazing at her, golden and beautiful in the soft thin dress. Tony, too, was the lover. The eyes that looked at Brook were as eyes that had loved Naomi, and his voice was to her like a remembered thing. Tony, and Brook's youth, all of that was on *her* side—on Joe's side. What chance had Caleb Evans to prevail against love and the years there were for love? "You don't owe him anything," she wanted to say to Brook. "Oh, don't worry. I have paid a price. I have paid your way." But she must not say it. She must be careful. Tony—it was Tony could speak for Joe. Youth to youth—and for it.

Then she remembered words she had been afraid to face. "How would you like to go to California, Brook?" California! As far from here as she was from the brook. She tried to consider what this house would be without Brook. It was a picture she had not the courage to make. "You can keep her," something whispered. "She is thinking of her duty to Caleb Evans. She will stay here with him—and you." She covered her eyes with her hand and let come music of a narrow stream far away. "No!" said Naomi. "No!"

CHAPTER XX

NAOMI and Brook sat in the parlor entertaining Mrs. Allen and her missionary daughter, Sylvia Waite.

This house had no sitting-room, and the parlor had remained a place to which one did not go unless there was company. There was almost never company, so the golden oak furniture was little more worn now than when it arrived from Denver that spring Brook was a baby. "Well, now we've got a parlor," Caleb had said, as he put in place the rocker, the big chair which did not rock, three smaller chairs, the table with fancy legs.

The dining-room had been furnished when she arrived. As they entered the house, after the long ride in the stage, and the drive from town over what seemed to her, and had remained, this flat and desolate land, Caleb said, "This room is all furnished." It had a table, a sideboard, four chairs shining with varnish. But they ate in the kitchen and the dining-room had not become a home-like room. There was no small worn rocker inviting you to sit by a window, no little low table to take here or there.

In their house was nothing from the past. It would be as expensive to ship things as to buy them new, Caleb thought—"so what's the use starting out with a lot of junk?" Nowhere did your head rest in a place worn by another head and your hand did not take hold of an arm smoothed by hands no longer there. Nineteen years had not smoothed or scuffed the golden oak into a home. Ashes had not been spilled from pipes, nor were there the only half rubbed out rings of glasses too cold or cups too hot. Quite different was her own home, the low house under the great trees. The wooden seats of chairs were rounded, stair rails were smooth, table legs battered, and old stains, but half worn away, were sometimes beautiful when the light moved over them.

How homesick she had been for that worn house, from which all had gone now save her baby brother. It was her own fault, her failure, she told herself, that she had not made this house a home. Only the things Brook had used seemed shaped by living. Brook—and John. The little bed and chair, the red wagon and hobby-horse, now in the dark of the upstairs closet.

Of these things she thought as she heard Sylvia Waite telling Brook how hard it was going to be to leave her home now that she had had it again.

Naomi did not like Mrs. Waite, but she was as nice as she could be to her to-day, because Brook

liked her. "Oh, they must be coming here," Brook
had cried, as they saw the white horse and phaeton
jogging along. "Could we make tea, Mother—
and bring it in on the tray?" "Of course," Naomi
assured her, "and those cookies will be nice." Poor
Brook, she so seldom had company that she felt
nervous about how things would go.

Mrs. Allen had been there when Brook was
born. There was no nurse, "But Mrs. Allen is a
good hand at such times," the doctor had said.
Naomi had been alone in the house, alone there on
the prairie, while Caleb (after one look at her face
as he came in he had said, "It's time?") went for
the doctor and the woman who would help. She
sat by the kitchen fire, knowing the time had come
for Joe Copeland's child to be born. And almost
as much as she felt the pain, she felt the strangeness
of it all. Now it was March. The wind shook a
small frame house alone on a wide high place beyond mountains. Joe was in his grave; but because there had been love in the summer nights
a new life was coming now, long afterwards, in
this far place.

To-day Mrs. Allen wore a black straw hat which
fastened under her double chin with white ties,
as if she felt she should be wearing a bonnet. She
must be near seventy now, but her pink cheeks and
wavy hair made her a pretty woman, comfortably
rounded by life rather than shriveled by the years.

That March day she came in with Caleb and the
doctor she wore a hood, which she took off without a word, and as she helped Naomi to bed she
had said, "Now, isn't it going to be nice to have
this over and done with, and your baby to keep
you company? Courage now—just a little longer!"
As if it were but a moment ago Naomi heard the
kindly voice saying this while the voice eighteen
years older said to Brook, "Yes, it is hard to give
up our children." "Oh, but you aren't giving me
up, Mother," said Mrs. Allen's daughter. "I am
doing what you would have me do. So we are
together in that." This voice Naomi did not like.
It was too confident. It knew nothing of the great
uncertainties that had shaped, or shattered,
Naomi's life.

But Brook had turned with pleasure to this buoyant assurance. As her child raised a fervent face
to the missionary Naomi realized that not alone
she and Joe were behind Brook. Maria Copeland,
Naomi's parents—just so would they have listened
to Sylvia Waite. "You know nothing!" something
within Naomi said passionately to the self-assured
woman. "Nothing!" And as if there were something for which she must speak, an obscure loyalty
which she at once knew as ill-advised, she said, a
little wildly, "Brook had such a good time at the
dance last night."

Brook turned sharply to her mother, then tried

not to give further sign of the anger her face had betrayed. In the .pause Naomi was trembling, as if the moment were more than her indiscretion and their polite disapproval.

"Oh, you dance?" said Sylvia Waite, as one who can be tolerant with all things.

"It's the first one I ever went to," said Brook.

Naomi tried not to say more, but Mrs. Waite's gently disapproving calm was a thing with which she was at war, as an evil influence near Brook. "A young girl should dance," she said, more aggressively than she had known it was going to be.

"Isn't it possible," asked Sylvia Waite, with the gentleness one employs toward an unreasonable person, "to put that—youthful feeling into the work we may do for our Lord?" She sat straight, confident and smiling, as to say, "See? Am I not happy? Has my Master's work not given me life?"

Naomi, bent, tense, could say no more, for she would say too much; but she felt with passion that while Sylvia Waite's face was smooth and hers drawn, while that life would seem full and hers not a successful life, felt that in her was the truth, and wanted words and power for the faith that had not died.

"Oh, Father!" Brook called with relief, as he passed the window.

Brook sat between Caleb and Mrs. Allen. It

was Mrs. Allen had taken Brook to Caleb. Naomi, lying above, heard her saying in the kitchen: "But you've not seen your daughter yet!" "Come down and see your father, young lady," she said as she bent to take the baby. Naomi tried to raise her hand. She whispered, "No! No!" "No?" laughed Mrs. Allen, with the tolerance that had met her again to-day. "A father not see his own baby? And such a lovely baby!" "I don't believe she's going to look much like her mother, and I don't see as she takes after you, either"—Naomi heard the words coming up as through a fog. "No," pierced the high voice of Caleb Evans, "I don't see as she does."

"You fold them this way," she heard Mrs. Allen tell him a few days later, for she must return home now and Caleb would have to take care of the baby.

That first hour they were alone in the house— she and Caleb Evans and Joe Copeland's baby, he came up with a glass of milk, spoke of a good fire in the kitchen, perhaps a baked potato for supper. He saw Naomi was nursing the baby and turned away. But he stood there. "You feel— stronger now?" "Yes," she answered, and added, "Thank you." He turned back to her. She wanted to say, "You have been good to me." The baby was hurting her breast. For that, or some other reason, she could not say it. He waited, then went slowly down the stairs.

He had been good to the pregnant woman. He slept in the little back bedroom, and she had been as alone as if she were again a girl in her father's house. But there came a night when he opened her door after the light was out. "No!" she cried in horror as he stood by the bed in his nightclothes. "No!" "God meant a man to be with his wife," he said, fervor made ugly by wanting long denied. To whom could she cry out? In all the world there would come no answer. She must pay now. This was what she had to pay—she who had known Joe Copeland!

Later that night, Caleb asleep beside her, the baby cried and she got up. "Brook!" she surprised herself by whispering, as she held Joe's baby against her. "Brook—Brook," she kept murmuring, as if it could cleanse her.

CHAPTER XXI

OF course she had never been fair to Caleb. "Bread, Father?" Brook asked gently, sitting at supper after Mrs. Allen and her daughter had gone. She said "Father" a number of times, lingering over the word as she had not done before. "Mother" she said only when she must, angry because Naomi had gone out of her way to speak of the dance. She and Caleb talked now, as often, about Sylvia Waite, "a grand woman." There was something tense in Brook's ardor. "Married you—and never let any one know? And never let *me*—" again Naomi heard, and remembered her daughter's eyes, like stars she had long ago seen in the brook.

"I don't mind doing them," she said, about the dishes, for she knew Brook did not want to be with her. On the back porch Caleb was studying the Bible lesson, as he did on Saturday evenings. Brook was looking up references for him—about Jeremiah. They were in the long twilight of a June night. It was in the twilight she had entertained Caleb on the porch at home, wanting him to go, because Joe would be waiting by the brook. But Caleb

would not go, not until he asked her to marry him
and come with him to this place where she had,
after all, spent nineteen years. How glad she had
been to get to Joe that night—the last night they
ever knew together. And what a joke Caleb had
seemed to them. "But you haven't told me—did
you accept him, Naomi?" The warm laughing
voice—so loving. "Did you accept him, Naomi?"
—bending her back, farther, farther,—his eyes, a
lover's laughing eyes—oh, so living!

"But, Father," Brook's sweet voice came, after
Naomi had finished in the kitchen and gone to the
flower-bed she had planted under Brook's window,
"don't you think it means—?" She did not hear
what it might mean. She did not care to hear.
Pinks that had been buds this morning were open
now, sending up an old fragrance. Sometimes all
dear old things were so deep in the past as to have
no reach into these days, but other times—a remembered smell in the twilight—it was as if love were
there waiting for her to go to it, after a bad dream.
She sat on a seat she had placed near the flowers,
looked across the wide valley to Big Chief, giving
back the light of a day that had gone.

She heard a horse, looked up to see a young
man riding across the valley. Tony was coming for
Brook! Once more a lover came through the twilight. She smiled as she heard Caleb and Brook,
still talking about Jeremiah. Soon Jeremiah would

be forgotten. And Caleb Evans, for the time, would be forgotten, until too much claimed Brook to leave ardor for this loyalty that denied life.

Brook could not see from where she sat, but she must hear him coming, she would have ears for this. He rode slowly, and it seemed the slowness of one who is sure, who would not too much hurry through the moment that brought him to happiness. Beautiful he was to Naomi, as healing to her own heart, making up for much. She had had her moment. Now there were other moments. This boy would not be riding to this love had there not been Joe. It was almost as if he were Joe, thus riding through the light sent down from Big Chief.

"Good-evening, Mrs. Evans." As he swung from his horse she went out to speak to him. His brown eyes were long—not wide, his features strong, straight—yes, something of the Indian. His voice had a softness, as from people who had lived in the South; it was almost caressing as he asked for Brook. Yet he was diffident.

He waited on the front stoop while she went to let Brook know he was there.

"Will you tell him," said Brook, not looking up from her Bible lesson, "that I cannot see him?"

"Why—Brook!" Naomi stammered, and stood looking at her daughter, whose eyes did not lift; then turned to Caleb, who was looking in surprise at Brook. "But you can't do that!"

"Why can't she?" asked Caleb.

"It's not kind. It's not fair. She—she doesn't want to."

"Will you give him my message, please?" said Brook, low, coldly.

"You must see him at least this once, dear. You must talk to him yourself and—"

"You urge your daughter to do what she thinks is wrong?"

"Wrong? Wrong to be decently polite? To see a friend who has—"

"Don't *argue* it," whispered Brook angrily.

In his slow way Caleb started to rise. "I'll tell him myself."

"No," said Naomi, "I will tell him." She waited, looking at Brook. "If it must be done."

But after she had started she turned back. "I think you are making a mistake, Brook." Seeing them there with their Bible lesson she added, "Is it so Christian to hurt a friend's feelings?"

Again Caleb moved as if to rise, so Naomi went where the boy on the front steps waited for Brook. He looked very long, stretched out that way, leaning on his arm, looking off at the mountain.

He sprang up when he heard footsteps, masked the eagerness that had leaped when he thought it was Brook.

"Tony," Naomi said, "Brook cannot see you this evening."

He waited, bewildered. "She—she's sick?"

Naomi shook her head. "No. It—it's her father."

Tony's face reddened; he stood more stiffly. Then he smiled uncertainly. "He didn't like it last night—about the dance?"

"That's it. He is very—well, too strict, I think, about such things. And Brook—"

He waited, wanting to understand, ready to be angry, hurt. "She feels to-night that she must obey him."

"But we aren't going to a dance to-night."

"No, but—"

"So it's me."

"It's on account of last night."

He bowed and was starting down the walk. She went with him. "I do not feel that way about it. Not—not at all."

"But Brook does?" he laughed.

"Because of a—because of something you do not know. It's something Brook—can't help."

He looked directly at her, for he would know, and in his eyes she felt how much it meant to him. "You—care for Brook?" she dared ask.

"I love Brook," he answered simply, with strength. "I want to marry her and take her with me to California."

California! Now Naomi could not speak. California. As far from here as— But while she stood there, dumb, the feel of the summer night passed over her like a message, like a command. "Then do not give up," she said. "This—this other—her father—that will pass."

"You do think she—likes me?" he asked, bashfully, twisting the bridle.

"I know she does," Naomi told him.

She sat on the stoop looking after him, he who would take Brook from Caleb Evans—and her. She watched until he reached the trees along the irrigation ditch, saw him riding before the willows. She, too, heard a stream near trees, but the stream she heard was a brook through meadows, the tree an oak. Big Chief was in between.

CHAPTER XXII

SHE heard the door of Brook's room close. The water was on for Caleb's Saturday night bath, which he took in the kitchen. He called to Naomi for towels. When she went in the shades were pulled, the tin washtub was in the middle of the room, on a chair the things Caleb would use, and he stripped to his under-drawers.

She always tried to avoid looking at her husband when he was not dressed, not alone for her own sake, but because it seemed unkind, like taking an unfair advantage. To-night she did look at him as she gave the towels, let him know that she was looking, for she would say to him, "And you —*you*—a miserably formed old man are standing between young lovers!" When he put the towel around his shoulders she was ashamed—either for what she had done, or for him, and went outside, where soft clouds hid and disclosed the stars.

After Caleb went upstairs Brook came from her room. Should she try to talk with her? No, not to-night. But she could not resist asking, "Did you want something, dear?"

"Only a drink of water," said Brook, her voice

excited, as if there was much she could scarcely hold back.

She wanted to know what Tony had said, but was too proud to ask. Naomi wanted to say, "Tony was so disappointed," but it would be better for Brook to speak of it herself.

She started back to her room, but finally came out on the porch, angry at being forced to ask, "Well, what did he say?"

"Why, he was disappointed, of course," answered Naomi.

"Can't you tell me what he said?" Brook demanded after a wait, and her mother smiled a little and took heart at the petulance. "What did *you* say?" she asked, as if the whole thing were her mother's doing.

"What could I say? That your father was angry about the dance, and so you could not see him tonight. It sounded rather foolish as I said it."

"I don't think it's foolish!" cried Brook. "I don't think it's foolish at all!"

Her mother made no reply. Having to talk, Brook came and sat on a step of the porch, just above her mother. She was in her nightdress, her light kimono over it. Her hair was unfastened and fell about her shoulders. "My baby!" Naomi wanted to say. "Brook—our baby!" she said within herself.

"If I should have to give my whole life to

Father," Brook was saying tensely, "that would not be too great a return for what he has done for me." At sound of her words she drew herself up, as in heroic feeling.

"Brook!" her mother whispered, frightened.

"I never," Brook went on, "*never* have known a more noble man."

That was what the others had said—over on the other side of this marriage, her mother and father, back home.

"When his own child—his son—his only child— was trampled before his eyes—out there—" Brook pointed—"even then he did not let me know I was no child of his." There was a pause. For the moment Naomi had no answer to this. "What must he have felt—don't you ever *think* of it—to have *me* here, his own child gone?"

"But he was glad you were here."

"And what about that?" Brook demanded. "Isn't that a spirit you owe something to? Oh, it isn't just for myself I must—make up to him. I must give him the gratitude—love—you never gave him."

"Oh, Brook!" her mother whispered. "Are you so sure you know—all about it?"

"As I think back to it now, I understand many things I had not understood."

"I wish you understood them all," her mother murmured. "If you understood them all— No, I

am glad you do not understand! Oh, no, I hope
you will never—never—"

"I can't see what Father has had from the sacrifice he made."

"Sacrifice?"

"Marrying you, and letting another man's child
pass for his."

Naomi laughed, quickly checked it.

"And—" Brook's voice was lower, but the feeling stronger— "there was never another child for
Father, to—make up for the child he lost."

Naomi did not know what to say. Too well
she could defend herself here.

"If you could know—" But she would not have
her know, and indeed covered her own face, as if
she herself would not again know. "Oh, you are
so *sure*," she cried, but quickly whispered, "Brook!
Darling!"

Brook's face was turned from her.

"Brook, dear," Naomi asked, "do you love
Tony?"

"And if I do," Brook answered, the voice less
steady than the spirit would have it, "it would be
just that much more to give up for Father."

Oh, what had she done? Last night—and long
ago? She saw herself, out beside the barn, there
at the chopping-block, trying to win her father for
love, as they threw sticks for Patsy to return—
telling her father she could not marry Caleb Evans,

knowing he should understand, indeed did understand. Blindly, but with some sure instinct, she was right in feeling the horror of this would be long. They said she must do it to save her child. She looked at Brook, sitting straight, hands now against her breast as if indeed an offering. Was it too late—too late to rescue her child from the man who had "saved" her?

"Your father—this man you call your father, and who married me because he wanted me, and could have me no other way—this man who took me when I was another's, and that other gone, whether he is good or bad, and he is some good and some bad, is an old man now, and you in your youth. These are the years that make your life. These are the years for love, and love is here. When he is dead, or in his dotage, and your youth gone, what will make up to you then, Brook, for the love you are letting go?"

Beautiful in her stern youth, Brook rose and stood there on the step, the love she denied going into fervor which let her say, "I think God will take care of that."

Naomi, who would rescue her daughter from this God cried, too wildly: "God is on the other side! He made the world and all its beauty, and through love He—"

But her daughter had left her.

CHAPTER XXIII

NAOMI did not sleep beside Caleb Evans that night. When at last she went up to their room, heard him there asleep, ugly in sleep, she was afraid to lie down beside him, fearing there would come a moment when she could be near him no longer and must rise and do some violent thing. She went to the little back room where Caleb had slept before Brook was born.

That thing Brook had said to her, reproach that there had not been another child for Caleb, would not let her sleep. It startled that her child should say it, for there were intimacies to which she and Brook had never drawn near. Because of the great secret she had not shared with her daughter there were even more than the usual barriers. When Brook was thirteen Naomi had told her what it seemed she should know. Eighteen now. Even though so much alone Brook would have gone beyond this talk, both in knowledge and in feeling about life. Now she could say, He cared for your child as his own, but you did not give him another after he had lost the child that was his. Yes, her daughter was coming into woman's knowledge, yet

how far short her knowledge stopped in understanding! And did Brook think it nothing to *her*
that their little son was killed before their eyes?
She hid her face, so much she had loved that frail
baby whose father she did not love.

Almost from the first, after the first horror of
having to be wife to him, she had wanted this child
for Caleb. That seemed to her right. She would
feel more self-respecting, as if she paid her way,
and Brook's way, in some other manner than
through the shame of the nights. As soon as she
was around after Brook was born she saw that
Caleb was interested in the baby, and because there
was no one else to whom she could talk of how
the baby could raise herself, how she played with
her toes and could hold with her fingers, she and
Caleb were talking of these things. They laughed
together the first time Brook threw the bottle she
had emptied; there would be moments, though
Naomi would not have believed this could have
become true, when amusements and pleasure shared
made them as parents enjoying their baby. Instead of being the awkwardness and the barrier
soon it was the baby gave them something of a life
together. Worries when Brook was not well,
thankfulness as an ailment passed, this at times
could bring the feel of home into their house.

They did not often have company, but when a
visitor from the church or a passerby would speak

to the baby of "your father," or to Caleb of "that
daughter of yours," this came to have a kind of
truth, until often she had not thought, and perhaps
he did not either, of how it was not true—so much
more powerful is living than anything which is shut
from living. It was in the hours she had alone
with her baby that Joe was Brook's father, and
again and again she would whisper things, giving
Brook to her father. Then Caleb would come from
work—"Well, young lady, been behaving yourself?"
or "Now—now," if she cried; would walk her up
and down while a bottle was heating, until it came to
be as if Brook had two fathers. She never dis-
trusted Caleb as father; after a little it did not
enter her mind that he would be hostile to the
baby's welfare, or even careless of it.

She could have come to feel friendly, loyal, perhaps something like affectionate toward him, had
it not been for those violations at night. Violations
they continued to be, for Joe was her lover, and
Joe was dead. There was something monstrous, a
defilement, in this grotesque and almost always un-
successful attempt of Caleb Evans to be man with
his wife. Naomi knew little of such things, but she
wondered if it weren't because he felt she was
thinking of Joe—comparing—that power would
desert him, and even though it was so hideous to
her that she would clench her hands, bite her lips
hard not to cry out, she was many times sorry for

him and wished she had power to make it otherwise. But caress, reassure, that she could not do, and he must know that she submitted with loathing. After such a night they were silent, trying to keep from one another next morning; then after a day or more had gone by, something from Brook—a smile, a long crying, would bring them together and for a time life was again possible—until once more she would know he was not going to sleep, that another hideous hour must separate them with resentment and shame.

Though there was no one to tell her, she came to feel it would be different if he could have a child of his own. His pride in that would make him a more confident man, she suspected. So she did herself try to take him into love, though it was like burying yourself deep and shamefully, as in a mad eccentric dream, making the gestures of life. It was those memories made her want to cry to Brook, "Oh, don't think I haven't paid your way!"

Then there was John. Strange days when she knew she bore Caleb Evans' child, at times bringing back into life those other days she was with child, that walk around the road from her house to Joe's mother's house. Joe's mother was still living at that time, was living yet, last Naomi had heard, sentenced by pride to a long old age in loneliness. Naomi had sent pictures of Brook back home, and she wondered if Maria Copeland ever

saw them. When the little girl laughed, or lay
sweet in sleep, Naomi would think of how Joe's
mother defeated herself, consider what the old
woman's life might have been with Joe's beautiful
child to watch and cherish.

Brook had outgrown her little chair and Caleb
said, "Guess I better put it out of the way." "Well,
don't put it too far out of the way," Naomi surprised herself by saying, for she had been wondering how she would tell him, wanting to let him know
and shrinking from the intimacy. He stood holding the little chair, looking at her. Any kind of
feeling threatened to make him absurd, so she
looked away, for she did not want to be thinking
that in this moment. He was helpless in the thankfulness that followed incredulity. "Well, *say*—"
he said in his high voice. He stepped nearer, as if
he would do something in showing his feeling. But
this was a thing that did not happen; never a caress,
or any intimacy between them except in the shameful dark. "We'll hope for a boy," she said, practically. A little later, "Oh, no, I'll do that for
you," when she went to bring kindling; and, "Here,
come bother me," he called to Brook when she was
jumping on and off her mother's lap.

She was wretched through those months; to-
night, alone in the little back room, considering it
all before Brook as judge, she knew it was not with
graciousness she bore a child for Caleb Evans. She

had not been equal to the two things—doing it, and doing it generously. Irritation, sullenness, were blight to his pleasure and struck at the pride with which she would have had this endow him. Once she said, "Oh, I'm sorry to be like this!" after her own pettiness was too hateful to her. He answered, "Guess a woman's not at her best, such times." There were times of hating to feel Caleb Evans' child within her, as if into her very body had come this life with him, and no matter what her withholdings she was now no longer her own.

"You have a son," Naomi heard Mrs. Allen say to Caleb. A tiny son, not a beautiful baby, like Brook. In this Naomi was sorry for the father. Little John was not strong. He cried as Brook had never cried. "That child never gives me a minute's peace!" She could hear herself saying it, fretfully. But when there were illnesses and they worked together with the baby all other things were less real than this which they shared.

And then came that horror and grief they shared. Though it could scarcely be said that here they shared. Caleb was a man stricken. He did not know what was happening to any one else, and she must take care of him as if he were a child—no, not a child, for a child's growing mind makes that care a satisfaction and delight. It was as if this had paralyzed Caleb—seeing, running against the threatened doom, and running in vain; carrying home his dying child. After that, though he could move, he was as one paralyzed.

In summoning a defense for herself to-night, though deep the hurt of her daughter's charge, it did not occur to her to use that winter on the side of what she had done for Caleb. There she did indeed give, and perhaps where one has wholly given one does not, even years afterward, use it to one's advantage. She helped him dress and undress; she would say, "Have you been outside yet?" for it was as if everything had stopped, and his body did not know how to care for itself. There had been times when she fed him. She would talk to him, as he sat looking straight ahead. One night in bed she put her arms around him and drew him to her. "There was never another child for Father". . . No, never another child. That life, which had ever been feeble, did not rally, though for a long time there was not acceptance of this and those memories she tried not to let come now— proof though they were, a hundredfold, that it was not she who denied Caleb Evans a child for the child he had lost.

Because those memories were too revolting she turned and looked out at the stars, trying to take refuge in the love she had known. That love had been brief, and to-night seemed far in the past. Joe's grave was an old grave now. Nearer, more

real, and sweet to her too, were the voice and eyes
of this boy who loved Joe's daughter. At last becoming sleepy, it was as if she were outside the
world, and the love of Naomi and the love of
Brook were both part of deep summer nights, which
passed.

CHAPTER XXIV

IN the month that followed Brook was much at
the Allens', helping Sylvia Waite, who would
not return for a number of years, prepare for
the long journey east of Constantinople. She was
getting ready her own clothes, also making things
for "some of the little ones." Brook had never
liked to sew, but now she not only worked with
Mrs. Waite and the others through the afternoons,
but brought home bright little calico dresses, sewing in the long twilights, her beautiful head bent
over her work, the lovely young face grave, with-
drawn. She usually sat on the back porch, seldom
using the seat her mother had placed near the flowers under her bedroom window. Caleb would call
to her from the kitchen, at times go out and sit
with her, and they would talk of things Sister
Waite had said that day, speculate on what little
girl would wear the dress Brook was making, what
it meant to the poor helpless children of a heathen
land to be cared for and brought to Jesus by this
grand woman. Brook was polite, kind to her
mother—a Christian sort of kindness, Naomi
thought bitterly.

One evening as she went into Brook's room with freshly ironed clothes, hanging the waist, she saw the sheer yellow dress Brook had worn but once. It hung there, in expectant grace, and Naomi put out her rough hand and touched it, as if she owed it to neglected beauty.

She felt outside, thwarted, troubled deeply, and with an anger that grew slowly, as from some deep place. The summer was passing, and she had felt it as she had felt no summer since that one which had taken her. Watching this new feeling between Caleb Evans and Brook, more than ever before he became to her all that denies life. There was, she found, much life left in herself. He was that which defeated. He was the enemy. She would come to, as from a dream, and find herself in the midst of canny plans for rescuing her daughter from him.

Did he know that Brook knew? Naomi would find Caleb looking at her, but she did not know what·was in his eyes, for they had little way of saying anything. Certainly he must wonder why Brook was so gentle—tender with him, when he was keeping her from life she wanted.

She had not gone back to the bed they shared for nineteen years. No word had been said. Here, too, he must wonder. But the truth of this he would not be likely to suspect. She was afraid to sleep beside him—hating him as she hated him now. No, that would be dangerous, for the nights became strange. She would wake from some old wanting; in the past she had thought, Brook will know what we knew. It will be again. Now—no, she would not dare wake and find herself beside him.

On her way home from Mrs. Waite's Brook had found a flower unlike any she had ever seen. They were talking about it on the porch as Naomi was getting supper. "Show it to your mother," he said. Naomi halted in her way from the stove to the table. It was as if he said, "Be good to your mother!" Caleb Evans asking Brook—*her* daughter—to take her into their companionship!

Brook came into the kitchen, holding out the stalk. "See, Mother," she said, with a cheerfulness not unlike Sylvia Waite's, "did you ever see such a shade of red? And the form, too—I wonder what it is?"

"Very strange," said Naomi shortly.

"Oh, *well*," said Brook, with resentment for having tried, and not been met, "if you're not *interested*." As Naomi did not reply: "I don't see any reason for being so disagreeable about things!"

"Oh, Brook," her mother murmured. "I don't want to be—I don't want to—"

But as it seemed her mother might cry, "Goodness!" Brook exclaimed, and went back to her father.

It was hard to sit through supper. "Am I to have her—have a little of her, now and then, as kindness from *him?*"

Tony was doing summer work at the agricultural school. When he finished this course—in August— he would go to California. There had been a letter from him, soon after the evening Brook refused to see him. Brook must have answered it, saying there could be nothing more between them, for he had not come there again, and Naomi had not seen other letters.

Would he let it go at this? Did the boy know no more than that? Would his pride keep him from trying to find out? She wished he could see Brook at times—in the long evenings—when she thought no one was looking. The good-night call of a bird, the first star—in that hour missionary fervor was not enough.

Brook had washed one of the little dresses which had blown from the porch and become dusty. She was outside taking it from the line at the side of the house. While watching her Naomi heard a horse, looked up to see Tony.

So he had come! There was shy warmth in her, as if his coming were for herself. Now Brook, too, saw him, almost in front of the house, and slowing. For an instant it seemed she did not know what to do. Then she felt the dress to make sure it was dry, began to unpin it. Tony halted. "Good-evening," he said. "Good evening," Brook replied, and turned to the house.

Her mother met her at the door. "Brook! Don't be so impolite! What are you thinking of? Don't be so silly!"

"Please let my affairs alone!" Brook answered, and in her agitation her mother saw how much it meant to her.

Naomi started past her. "I'll—"

Brook caught her wrists. "Will you mind your own business!" It seemed she would strike her mother.

For the moment there had been no sound outside—now sound of a galloping horse.

"You're a fool!" Naomi found herself saying.

"I'm not what you were!"—passionately, with anger that must be hatred, Naomi's daughter faced her, then threw the dress on a chair and went hurriedly to her room.

Weak now, Naomi leaned upon the table in the kitchen, sat down. That she and Brook could speak to each other like this!

It was almost dark; Caleb had gone to bed; Brook did not come from her room. Naomi continued to sit without moving; it grew dark, and still she did not move. That she and Brook could face each other like that—saying those words! And why—*why?* Why? Because of Caleb Evans —that half-alive old man asleep upstairs. He had taken Brook—from her, from life. What could she do? How save her daughter?

She wished he were dead. He might live years and years. She wished she could keep him from living through those years that should be years of life for Brook.

She knew now how much Brook wanted Tony. In those angry eyes, she saw it. And because she wanted him much, it was that much more to give to this loyalty before which she was laying down her life. Oh, the foolish girl! Stubborn—brave—good—*good* Brook!

Yes, some one else must do it for her. She must be rescued—that would be the way. Naomi herself might die. Caleb Evans would live on—on—and on. She saw it happening, saw him old—wickedly old, and Joe's daughter ministering to his needs.

She must not let that happen. It was Brook she must think of—not him—not herself.

Other women had done as much. Why could not she? Was there anything in this world she would not do for her little girl?

But as she tried to think what she could do she was not alone in this dark kitchen, in an ugly house on a prairie beyond the mountains. She was in the kitchen back home. Father would come in in a moment, with Patsy. Mother must be upstairs, putting Willie and Rosie to bed. If she lighted the

lamp she would see the pans hanging around the
stove. The sink was behind her, and bread set on
the table over there. Home. And the security of
home. She wanted it! She did not want to do
this lonely, lonely thing—more lonely than all her
life. "Father!" she whispered. "Father—help
me! O Heavenly Father—*you* help me!"

She could not be alone any longer. She went
toward Brook's room. Outside the door she heard
low sounds. Brook was crying. For years she had
gone to her when she was crying. She could not
go to her now, could not go to her any more than
if this were a door which did not open. She must
save her from the door which did not open! No
matter how, must save her.

She went back in the kitchen and lighted the
lamp. On the table were tablet and pencil—Caleb
had been writing to the mail order house in Denver.
Their long knife—he had been sharpening the
pencil. She felt the pencil-point. Yes, it was sharp.
Sharp? Sharp! She lay her finger on the knife-
blade. Sharp—oh, yes, it was sharp! Suddenly she
snatched it and opened the stair door.

He was snoring. She stood and listened, feeling
a little crazy, knowing she was not really crazy but
was only brandishing the knife as if she were. Feeling crazy and knowing she was not, she stood at the
foot of the stairs. For years and years he had
snored, and she had listened. There came the

idea that because she knew this about him, she must
protect him. Must protect him from all the things
she knew about him. You could not harm a man
you could reach in his sleep. In sleep we are de-
fenseless. Every time we go to sleep, we are trust-
ing those around us. Other nights she had wakened
him from his snoring. "Quick! Brook has colic!"
she would whisper. Or, "John is choking!" How
quickly he, a slow man, would be out of bed!

The knife fell from her hand. Sobbing, she
bent low. "I can't! I can't! O God, forgive me,
I cannot!"

After long crying, she was again by the table.
She was fingering the pencil. Suddenly it began
to write. *"Dear Tony—"* it wrote.

CHAPTER XXV

PERHAPS he would not be there. She had given the letter to one of the cattle men passing the house next morning. He might have forgotten to mail it. Or Tony might have gone back to school. As she waited for Caleb to go to bed, Brook to go to her room, where she read or worked now in the evenings (since that last encounter she did not speak to her mother if she could help it) Naomi fortified herself with all the reasons why Tony would not be waiting for her down by the willows. She gained strength for what she wanted more than she had wanted anything in nineteen years—perhaps more than she had wanted anything in all her life, by telling herself it was not to be.

It was as it had been long before—waiting for the others to go to their rooms. It grew darker, and she was going for a secret meeting. How could old excitements live so long? She did not feel old—shattered. It thrilled and frightened her that the life long smothered by living could thus leap into an old situation, not knowing differences, but after long waiting, now ready.

Walking down the road she did not try to break
the spell; as if, after having been long dead, one
has the gift of a moment of life. It gave Joe, too, a
moment of life. Time enough, if Tony should be
there, to face what she had to do. Now the loved
hour, the old pattern of it, made her Naomi, and
she went slowly, as if a little ahead of time, lifting
her face to the fragrant breeze, letting the dark
deepen, that it might take her, knowing in the il-
lusion the beauty, meaning, of the reality. There
had been shameful years; to-night she walked
through the dusk as through that which cleanses.

She heard water flowing under trees. She covered
her eyes, that there might not be the differences, but
letting the old sound take her farther into the old
beauty. If she had held out her arms . . . ?
"Naomi—" he would whisper. "Naomi!"

It was a shock when she saw Tony's horse among
the trees. Could she turn back? Would it not be
as if she had only turned back from the love to
which she would return? She could not break the
spell to-night when, perhaps more than ever before,
she had what she had lost.

Yet something in her knew it was not safe to return to that house, nothing changed. She must free
Brook. She must do it this way, instead of that
other way. The pencil had been there, when she
dropped the knife. And now Tony had answered

her. Now she must do it—*this* way—so she would not have to do it that other way.

As she stepped up to him, curious indeed how quickly she could become Brook's mother. "This is a strange place for us to be, isn't it, Tony?" she laughed, to put him more at ease. "But I did not want Brook or her—or Mr. Evans to hear what I have to tell you."

What she had to tell him. That was it. That was why she was here, in the night, by the stream that murmured under trees. Well, now she must tell him. *This* way—not—not another way.

"Brook is unhappy," she began.

He laughed, the laugh of one so much hurt he must scoff.

"Then why does she act like this?" Naomi asked for him.

"Yes," he returned. "Why?"

"I have come to tell you why."

Hard—hard to tell it; that was because, walking down the road, she had again lived it. The change from Naomi to this woman—Brook's mother—had come too quickly.

Very well then, let *that* Naomi tell it. Not the woman who had told it to Brook, but the girl who had lived it. The dark would help her, let her, for a moment, be that other Naomi. The sound of the water within the sound of the trees, as an inner, a secret sound. As it was before—as it was in the beginning—is now—and ever shall be!

She moved nearer and looked into the water. "Oh!" She pointed to the reflected star. "It used to be there.

"There was a brook. As it is now with you and Brook, for my father said No. But, No? What is any one else's No, when you are young, and love?"

She was telling him. They were seated—a fallen tree was there for them, and he leaned toward her, not moving. "Joe is Brook's father."

She looked now, not at him, but into the stream, not because she was embarrassed, but thinking of Joe as Brook's father. "He should have lived," she murmured, thinking, not of herself, or of Brook, but of Joe.

"It was only the other night, when you came home from the dance, that I told her.

"So you see," said Naomi, "what has happened?"

If he did see, he waited for what she would add.

"She feels she owes him more than if he were her father."

"Of course," he murmured, as if this cleared something for him.

"She doesn't owe him her life, does she?" Naomi asked sharply.

Instead of answering, "Yes, Brook would be like that," he said softly.

"And you think there is nothing to do about it?"

"Oh, I wouldn't say that," he laughed, and something joyous, young—rough, took his voice. She saw that he was smiling. Strength. Strength seemed all through him. Brook, not she, should be here now.

But how would he reach her, for Brook was "like that." When she and Joe met by the brook they brought with them all that was behind them. The Kelloggs. Maria Copeland too.

Why—just why—was she here? Now she had told him, yet what had she to say to him? Alone he could not do it, for he could not reach Brook. Now she knew she had come to say something which she had not said to herself. What was all this for, if not this thing she had come to say? But just then, making it too hard for her to say it, she began to realize how she must look. There was a bunion on one of her feet, and when she put her hand down to it, she realized her ugly, worn lace shoes. She wore a coat she made from the coat she had not wanted Brook to wear any longer. The sleeves were too short, her misshapen hands stuck out in a way that suddenly made anything she could say— as if not quite right in her mind. She had tied a veil round her head but it had blown loose and her hair was blowing in her eyes. When hair is thin, graying, made harsh from little care in a dry country—she tried to pin it back, but knowing now how she must look, how could she say—what indeed she had never told even herself she had come to say?

It was he who indicated it. "I will have to— rescue Brook. I must—"

Must—*what?* Brook's mother did not like the way he laughed. Was it easier to go far in his thoughts because of what she had told him? Now that he knew she herself had not waited for marriage did he think . . . For some reason she liked him a little less now. For the first time she felt uncertain. So great had been her other fears she had scarcely known the usual mother fear. Brook, her little girl, safe there at home, unsuspecting. This boy—why did he now seem different? Was he, after all, half good enough for Brook? What was she putting in his mind! She—a mother.

She lifted her face and sought old reassurances.

"You will help me?" he was asking. "Together we will—rescue her?"

That was as she had herself thought it. Why then did she not accept it now? She felt excitement in him. He was a stranger—with the instinct for his rough purpose. And Brook, the baby soft against her breast—the tender flesh—that dear little girl. The days they had had together in this lonely place, while Brook had so sweetly—so purely— grown older—her baby—and Joe's.

Yes, and Joe's. Joe, who was dead, but who had lived.

"Then we will be married," said the boy, reasonably, "and go to California."

Of course. Just so had she, too, thought it out.

"You came—to help me?" he pressed. "You will arrange that I can see Brook when her father— is not there?"

It was indeed what she had come to arrange. The following week Caleb would go into the mountains, where their sheep were. Tony would come. She would shut herself in her room, might even have a sudden call over to their neighbors, the Scotts. And when Brook knew more about love. . . .

"I will let you know," she said. She was cold. Her hands hung there graceless. She tried to slip them into the sleeves of her coat. But the coat did not protect her. Nothing protected in this moment.

"How?" he asked. "How will you let me know? Soon I will be leaving for California." He was persistent, almost sharply persistent, it seemed. She had to think quickly—something that would let her do it or not do it. She would leave a note, she told him, under a stone by the gatepost of this southern boundary. It sounded so fantastic she had to laugh, quickly checked this, for if she heard her own laugh —so easily it could all seem crazy.

He turned for his horse, but came back. Hesitant, he seemed just a boy—uncertain, awkward. "Gee, it was good of you," he said.

"Good-night," she said.

"You're cold."

"Never mind!" She was striving against panic.

"I—can't I help you get home?"

"No! No, I'm going in a minute," she added, more quietly. "I always liked to—sit beside running water."

Again he waited uncertainly, then left her.

She did not move until the sound of the trees was between her and the sound of his horse. She found herself so stiff it was hard to rise. As one crippled she started away, but she turned back to the stream. She wanted to see the reflected star.

But the star had changed its place in the heavens, and was no longer reflected on her earth.

CHAPTER XXVI

"WISH I was going with you, Father. I'd love a week in the mountains."

"Ought to have thought of it sooner. Well, maybe. You could have the littlest hut and we men folks— But your mother'd be here alone."

"Mother isn't afraid here. But I can't go, really. It's Sister Sylvia's last week."

The Scotts would come by for Caleb at daybreak. Brook had been helping him get ready. "I'd wear the thinner wool socks, but take the heavier ones along. You know the nights up there. You must be careful, Father. You'll keep the sheepskin on all the time, won't you?"

"She's fussy as an old woman," said Caleb to Naomi, pleased.

Brook was about to say good-night, she would not be up at four.

"If I'm not back in time to say good-by to Sister Waite, you give her my—my best wishes. Tell her I will always pray for her safety."

"Yes, Father."

At second mention of Sylvia Waite Naomi went into the front room. This whole hour of ministra-

tions and friendly exchanges had been hard for her.
She heard Caleb saying something in a lower voice:
"Good to your—" And Brook reply dutifully,
"Yes, Father."

Be good to your mother! That was what he had
said.

"It's too bad we didn't think sooner about my
going. I could cook for you."

"Well—" Caleb laughed, and Brook joined him.
Brook did not excel as a cook. But on what good
terms they were! How she hovered about, thinking
of his comfort! This could become her habit. In
her stern young way she would take him unto herself
as her charge. Naomi thought of Maria Copeland's
cousin, the spinster who opened the door for her
that day she came to tell about Brook. Many
women like that in the world; even to a beautiful
young girl it could happen, if through an idea of duty
she turned away when life was there. "We must
rescue her," she heard Tony saying. Yes, must
rescue her. Even against her own fears, even not
knowing what might be ahead. Something that was
life would be ahead—better that, whatever it might
be, than the path farther and farther away from
life. So she thought, hearing Brook's sweet voice
in good-by to Caleb Evans.

"Take good care of yourself."

"Yes. You do the same. And you take good care
of your mother."

"I will, Father," said Brook gravely.

A pause, then a movement. She had kissed him good-by.

"Good-night," said Caleb, touched by her affection, for there had been few kisses in that house.

"Good-night, Father," said Brook, lingeringly.

With something that was almost gloating, and of which she was ashamed, Naomi thought—perhaps it is good-by indeed!

He was still in the kitchen when she went to leave breakfast things handy, for there would be little time in the morning. He was closing his canvas bag. Other years it had been Naomi who gave final precautions—warm clothes, go carefully if he had to do climbing. It seemed Brook had said all that this time.

"Well, guess I'll be getting to bed," he said.

"I'll take the alarm to my room so I can—" She faltered. It was the first word had been said of her room.

"Guess I could get my own breakfast."

"Oh, no. I'll be up, and call you."

He lighted his lamp to go upstairs. Turned from her he ventured: "Well, maybe you and Brook'll have a good time here together. Kind of like a visit—just you two."

Tears surprised her; even though he had not turned to her she turned her back. Words she so sorely needed—but could not accept from him.

It was Brook who established the kind of visit
they would have while there alone, as if she were
the older person, determining the place in which they
were to move. There were to be no disagreeable
encounters, for these are a part of intimacy, and may
open doors to what is there. There was to be pleas-
antness, consideration, but all this within a restricted
place. This Naomi felt her daughter's manner say
to her as they did the work together next morning.

In her need she took the offered crumbs; as if it
were some dangerous game, disaster just outside,
she would play that a polite offer of assistance was
love. As Brook moved about the house with her
she could at moments forget how it was between
them and make a world in which they were indeed
mother and daughter.

Naomi would be upstairs and hear Brook moving
around below—light step she knew so well. Outdoors she knew she would find her little girl in the
house. She would cook for Brook, iron her clothes,
and Brook would say, "How nice it is," or "Thank
you, Mother," and she could half let herself feel
this was expression from a feeling that need not
express itself in fulness.

The afternoon of that first day Brook sewed on
the little dresses. Naomi, passing through the room,
saw the sunlight make gold her hair. She was here!
However it might be between them—she was near.
What would life be if she were out in the yard and

knew she would not find Brook in the house? If she waited within, knowing Brook would not come home? Had she not seen things all wrong? Brook was not Naomi. Did she not have the right to shape life as she wanted life for herself? Perhaps from this, after a time, would come something that was right for Brook. And meanwhile—she would be here! In the daily life together, differences would wear away. She would be so good to her, and so careful, that she would have her again—for a time— for yet a little longer!

So it would present itself, as the sun went toward the West. After this sun had set she must leave word for Tony, unless she make no further effort to send Brook from Caleb Evans—and herself.

Twilight now, and Brook had gone to her room. Naomi had been out seeing that the little chickens were secure, was giving water to the flowers when she heard sounds from Brook's room. She went nearer. Smothered sobbing. Passionate, deep. Naomi stood and listened—hearing what was there, underneath that control.

She heard another sound. Mrs. Allen's phaë- ton. Sylvia Waite was coming to see Brook.

Naomi hurried in. "Brook! Brook dear! Mrs. Waite is coming to see you!"—for she must give her a moment to bathe her eyes.

"Goodness!" Brook cried, in the old exaspera- tion.

No, Mrs. Waite could not come in; she had only driven over with a message about to-morrow. While Brook was out talking with her Naomi opened the door of her daughter's room. Crumpled on the bed, as if clutched by unhappy hands, was the yellow dress Brook had worn to the dance.

Outside she could hear Sylvia Waite's voice and Brook's acquiescence. She moved nearer the dress, twisted, marked with tears. She put her own hand upon it, as if seeking strength for what she had to do.

CHAPTER XXVII

NEXT evening Naomi, sitting by the kitchen table mending for Caleb, would raise her eyes to the clock. A quarter past seven. Between half-past seven and eight Tony would be expecting to find Brook at the bars of the pasture. It would be better so, she had thought, than for him to come here, where Brook's stubbornness against her mother would be another reason for refusing to see him. He would "just happen along," tell her, perhaps, that even to be near her house was something to him—oh, he would know what to tell her, one did not distrust him there. "I am going away," he would say. "What have I done? You must talk to me—tell me—before I go away." She would stay with him a moment. "I love you!" he would say. She would cry and he would comfort and plead with her.

"Oh!" Naomi exclaimed. "Oh, *dear*. Now isn't that too bad!" And she rose with even more difficulty than she felt.

Brook, pressing the last of the little dresses, looked up.

"I forgot to fasten the bars when I took the

mash down for Blossom and Spot. I can't remember putting the pail down after I went through. Yes, I know I forgot!"

"Oh, Mother!" Brook reproached.

"Well," sighed Naomi, "I'll just have to go back." She moved toward her coat, again sighing heavily, lifting her feet as if they hurt.

"I'll go," Brook said, with patience.

"Oh, no, dear, you're busy. And it serves me right."

"I will go," Brook repeated, putting the iron on the stove. She started to her room, turned back, holding out her hand. "Let me take your coat."

Naomi held it out, but withdrew it. "Better get your cape. I got this soiled, working in the barn."

Brook had not changed her dress since she came home from the meeting at Mrs. Waite's. She was lovely in her flowered muslin.

Naomi followed her outside. "Sorry, dear. It's good of you to go for me. If you should like being out, feel like a little walk, and wanted to go on over to the Scotts'—maybe they've heard something from the men."

"Oh, I don't think so," said Brook. "Not yet."

"Just as you like," said Naomi, hastily. She followed a step or two down the path. "It's a nice night," she said, out of a great timidity, longing to reach out her arms to her daughter, keeping her, and longing to tell her to go, tell her not too quickly to turn back.

She watched Brook go into the dusk. Going—to what was she going? Perhaps Brook would suspect an arrangement, and then she would be more angry than she had yet been with her mother, more than ever resolved to devote her life to her father. But if Tony managed it right—no, she would not be likely to suspect. She would stay with him a moment, they might walk down by the willows. "I must go back," Brook would say. "Mother will be worried." "No," she would consider, wanting to stay, "she will think I have gone to the Scotts'." So they would perhaps go over to the Scotts'—Brook not wanting to say she had gone there if she had not. They would go together, but Tony would not go in with her. She would stay a moment—but it could seem at home she were staying an hour. So Naomi had thought it out for Brook.

She finished the little dress Brook had been pressing. "You did my work, so I did yours," she would say, and wishing she herself could do the missionary side of it, all that part of life for her child. The dress was like dresses she had ironed for Brook. If she looked around, would she not see Brook playing with a doll? Would there not any moment come a baby voice: "Mamma! Brook's hungry, Mamma!" Naomi's tears fell to the pink calico. She would not be ironing these little dresses again.

Yet, might she not—sometime—for Brook's little girl? Oh, there must be that little girl—sweet baby voice—not barren years with Caleb Evans.

It was half-past eight. If Tony had not understood, and Brook had not met him, or if she had refused to linger with him, she would be home now. If she did meet him, and turn from him, then she would not go to the Scotts'. No, she would run home, to be secure against him, against herself, would go to bed and sob for the love she denied herself. It was a quarter of nine. They were together!

Naomi sat on the steps of the back porch, that she might be in this summer night which offered love to her daughter, as if she were sending out all that she knew, everything she had felt, to give the night more power.

But now it was twenty minutes of ten. She was beset by fears that can come while waiting, no matter what sympathy there may be with the absence. Suppose something had happened to Brook? She might not have met Tony at all—or, she might have met him. . . . What did Naomi know about this boy, except that he wanted Brook? Now she was afraid, and she wanted to run down the path her daughter had taken, bringing her safely back to this house. Brook might be in danger! And as another half-hour went by, Naomi Kellogg was braver than she had ever been in her life. Brook might be in danger—and wanting to go and find her, she sat where she was, for while she could take her into a house in which there was not danger, it would be a house in which there was not life. She knew— what things could happen. Old fears, sorrows, shame, all said to her, "Run down that path." But there were other memories. Here was the hour when she was on the one side or the other. The danger she had braved for herself—was she brave enough to encounter it for her child? Did she *believe* enough? "Anything that life can do to you is better than not having lived." She spoke it as her creed. But she could no longer look into the large darkness. She went into the house to wait for her little girl to come home.

Past ten she heard running footsteps. "That you, dear?" she called, knowing the worry in her voice would not serve her ill.

"Were you worried, Mother?" Brook asked. Her excited voice had a new freshness, and Naomi knew.

"Beginning to be." She did not at once come down into the lighted room, giving Brook a moment to adjust herself to the house. How well she knew the strangeness of those returns!

"You went over to the Scotts'?" she asked after Brook had gone into the hall to hang her cape.

"Yes. They haven't heard from the men yet. They thought if I came over to-morrow night. . . ."

So there would be a to-morrow night!

"Something hot to drink, dear?" Naomi asked, as Brook came into the kitchen.

"No,"—holding her hands over the fire. "Well, maybe; yes, some hot milk."

Did Brook think it was the same voice? Naomi, turning for the pan, delayed in choosing it, knowing she had won, and lost.

CHAPTER XXVIII

IT was on the third day after this Brook began going through her things.

"You know,"—she brought out a skirt to press— "I haven't really been through my things for a long time."

At first her mother could make no comment. "That's so, isn't it?" she agreed, when she had finished what she was doing.

"So busy in school—I've just neglected everything."

Naomi went upstairs and remained there half an hour.

When she came down Brook was energetically examining stockings, making ready to run ribbon in underwear.

"I'll tell you, dear—while Father's away is a good time for us to get your things really in shape." (Yes, her voice was all right now. Yes, she could go through with it.) "Let me wash out anything that needs it."

"Why, would you, Mother?" Brook asked uncertainly.

"Of course," said Naomi, practically; but could not refrain from adding: "Of course—darling."

So they got Brook's things ready—hung on the

line, sponged, brushed, without ever letting come
into words that this was going to change life for
them both.

"I must not! I must not!" Naomi would tell herself when she longed to say: "Mother wants you to
be so happy, darling. The only thing Mother wants
in the world—" No! She would turn away, but,
her back turned, tears would fall to the thin white
things she washed—handkerchiefs, pieces of underwear given Brook as presents, and cherished. So
few of them! And she longed to give her the finest,
loveliest things there were in the world. Afraid of
all she was feeling she would say cross things.
"Brook! Don't be so slow out there." Or, "For
pity's *sake*—don't let that stew burn!" Irritated
things she would say, to make it easier for Brook.

A couple of nights Brook had gone over to the
Scotts'. Naomi, longing to see her when she came
in, would only call down from upstairs. The second
night she rather fretfully said: "It must be after
nine, isn't it?" when she knew it was past eleven.
Last night, as soon as the supper dishes were out of
the way, Naomi said she had a headache and was
going to take one of those powders and go right to
sleep. "So I'll say good-night now," she said—and
later she heard them softly moving about downstairs.

She wished she dared say: "Why don't you ask
Tony to come over one evening while we are alone—
so you can explain why you had to hurt his feelings

like that?" But this she was afraid to do. Brook was deceiving her father and was going to leave him, but she would not bring into the open the fact she had taken sides with her mother against him. And even with this better feeling between them she knew that underneath Brook was still stubbornly set in disapproval of her, and Naomi would not risk associating that feeling with the thing Brook was herself doing. Any time through those next few days of knowing she was losing Brook she could have kept her by saying: "Mother understands." Because she loved her, she kept the gulf between them. And she knew she must guard her strength for that hour when she would know Brook was leaving, and she would not be able to say "Good-by," to say "Be happy," to say, "God bless my darling."

Naomi would see her moving about the house, pausing before her father's things, hurt by the unhappiness she was going to bring him. She wanted to say: "I will be good to your father. When you are gone, dear, I will be better to him than ever before—will take care of him for you." Unable to say this, though she was indeed feeling, planning it— for she would have won, and so could be generous, she would do as much as she dared indirectly. "I want to have everything nice for Father when he gets back. These trips are hard for him—I think he ought to give them up, and take it easier now." "Yes, Mother," Brook would say, "I think he should have it easier now." "We'll have chicken for him on Sunday," she said, then heard Brook go swiftly from the room.

Brook would not be there on Sunday!

"Would you be afraid here alone, Mother—all night?"

Naomi was peeling potatoes. Her hands stopped just as they were. Brook was going to-night!

"No, I wouldn't be afraid." But, oh, how afraid she had been that her voice would not be this natural voice.

"I want to go this afternoon to tell Sister Sylvia good-by. You know she's leaving to-morrow. And then I thought—maybe I'd like to go on into town— to Madge Atkins'. She—she's having company."

Hard for Brook to tell an untruth. "That will be all right," said Naomi, head bent over her work.

Then to-night she would not lie listening for Brook to come home. Yes, she would lie listening, but Brook would not come. No one would be moving around downstairs. She would come down in the morning, but not to get breakfast for Brook. After to-day would she ever again hear her voice, look into her eyes? And she could keep her—oh, so easily, could keep her with the words, "Darling, Mother understands."

But within herself Naomi said: "Now I have come to what I fought for. This is the meaning of all my life! I will be strong this day, and then all the days of my life it will not matter—what I am. Not me! Brook! "Not *you*," as if indeed pushing herself aside. "Not you—Brook!"

She found that a number of Brook's clothes had gone. They must have been taken away the night before.

"But where will you be married, darling?" she longed to ask. "Will some one be with you?" Oh, if she could be with her! But no—on her mother's side then, against her father. In spite of this thing she did, Brook was on her father's side, and this must be guarded for her.

She and Brook sat down to their last meal together.

"A few more of the cherries, dear?" When again would she offer her child from the good things she could have for her? What would she do now when she saw things that would be as an offering for Brook? "Well, I will send them to her," something practical in Naomi came to her rescue, as she handed the cherries to Brook.

Brook did not finish eating them; abruptly she left the table. For Brook, too, it was hard, and she dared not go to her with comfort. The only help she could give her was in getting her away quickly, without emotion.

Now Brook was getting dressed in her room.

"Shall we harness Bess and I drive you over to Mrs. Allen's?"

"No, Mother. No." Brook did not want the ride with her.

"I'll tell you," said Naomi, a little later. "I really have lots to do, but you take Bess, and get their boy to drive her back. I'll pay him for it."

Brook hesitated. "No, I don't mind walking." She wanted to get away.

A stage left town at six o'clock, connecting with the night train west. Brook would leave in that—Tony meet her somewhere along the way; they would take the train together. But where would they be married? Here? At the Junction? Not till they got to California? Worry about that later—leave that till later—and Brook would see that all was right.

"It doesn't seem very nice of me," said Brook from the other room, "leaving you here alone."

"Oh, I don't mind," said Naomi. "I'm not a bit afraid, and I want you to—to have a—good time."

Brook, all ready to go—her blue suit, the hat with rosebuds—came into the kitchen. "You always did want that, Mother."

For this Naomi was unprepared. Yet she met it. "Oh, mothers are like that," she said. "They're just—made that way. I never could understand why they—took any credit for it."

A silence between her and Brook—in that kitchen where they had been through the years of Brook's life, and would not be again.

Striking at a longing that could not grow bigger and be held back, "Well, better be along, dear," she said.

But Brook came up to her. "As I'm leaving you here all alone I'll—" She put her arms on her mother's shoulders, raised her face to be kissed.

No! Hold back—hold back! Not too much. Only as if for the night! But she did dare put her arms around her little girl—her baby—Joe's—put her arms around her as she kissed her good-by.

"Well," laughed Brook, wiping her eyes, "I'm not a person that stays away from home much, am I?"

"No, darling, you've been here with me—so much. Now you have a good time!" she said, in an almost violent voice.

"Good-by, Mother."

"Good-by—Brook."

No, she would not go outside. She would not look after her. She would *not.* But she did. And, as through the years she had gone to school, Brook turned and waved. Naomi waved back, then pressed her hands tight against her breast. Brook turned again and this time she threw a kiss—something she had rarely done since she was a little girl. Pressing both hands passionately against her mouth, Naomi sent the kiss with arms extending far—reaching as far as they would go toward the child her arms would not know again.

CHAPTER XXIX

JUST before dark of the second day following Naomi heard horses, and looked out to see the wagon in which Caleb was returning with the Scotts. They came slowly, for the horses were tired; and Caleb looked very tired, bent, hands hanging at his sides. Naomi moved the supper she was keeping for him from the back to the front of the stove, stirred the fire. Perhaps she could let him think Brook had gone to bed, not tell him until he had eaten, perhaps not tell him until he had slept. She was sorry for him as she saw him sitting there, stiffly bent. Now that she had defeated him she wanted to be gentle. It wasn't only that he would be disappointed in Brook, but how he would miss her—for he had always loved her.

"Well, you got back," she said in a voice perhaps too bright.

"Yes, back again." And as she heard his voice she looked at him sharply. He must be cold and tired out. "Sit here by the fire while I fix your supper," she said. He sat down stiffly.

"Cold? A little ginger tea? I've got it here."

"No—no. Yes, it was cold—sitting there so long."

She got his food ready, looking at him apprehensively as he held shaking hands toward the oven. "These trips are too hard for you," she said.

"Yes, getting old. Old. How are you?" he asked suddenly.

"Oh, I'm all right." Now he would say, "Where's Brook?" But his head sank and he did not ask for Brook.

She had his supper on the table. "All ready," she said, but he continued to sit before the fire. He must indeed be exhausted; she had never seen him like this. "Maybe you'd like to eat right here by the stove," she suggested.

For the moment there was no kind of response, then he started, as if only then reached. "No. No," he said in his high nervous way, only more feebly than ever before. "Oh, I'll come to the table." Like a very old man he moved over to his chair.

She waited on him, but she did not sit at her place, for that would leave Brook's place an emptiness between them.

He opened his baked potato, took some of the beef and gravy she had prepared as he liked it. But he was not eating, he was watching her, whenever he thought she was not looking. Suddenly he put down his knife and fork.

"Well, guess I may as well tell it."

He tell it? *What?* What had *he* to tell?

Naomi stood by the table waiting.

"Can't seem to eat anything—do anything—until I tell it."

He had heard in town!

Naomi sat down across the table, Brook's empty place between them. "No need to tell it," she said.

He leaned a little forward, hands gripping the edge of the table.

"No need to tell it?"

"No need to tell it," she repeated. "I know."

"You know? No. No, you do not know."

"Brook has gone," she said.

"Yes."

"She left with Tony."

"No."

Had something happened to his mind? His head shaking back and forth like that. Naomi waited for him to recover himself.

"She left with Sister Waite," said Caleb.

She stared at him. He had it all wrong. He had heard a little and got it mixed. Of course that was it! But why was it she now who, deep inside herself, was shaking so?

She must put this straight at once!

"She has been seeing Tony."

"Yes."

"She thought I did not know."

"Yes."

"But I did know."

"Yes."

Why did he keep saying "Yes—Yes," when he had it all wrong?

"She left here to meet Tony, to be married, to go West with him."

"Yes."

"Yes,—yes!" she fairly screamed back at him. "Yes!"

"But—you'll have to bear it, Naomi. I know it's not what you wanted. She changed her mind before she left. She—" He reached in his pocket, started to draw out a paper. "No—no, I can't do that!"

She was over at his side of the table. "Give me that!"

"It's for me."

"Give it to me—before I take it from you! Give it to me! Give it!" until he could do nothing but let her take it from his pocket, he whimpering: "I hadn't meant to. She hadn't meant you to. It's too *hard* for you. *Don't* read it—I'll tell you—"

But Naomi had smoothed out the paper and was reading:

"Dear Father: I will not see you again. Maybe not for a long time. I had a great temptation, and I was going to do what you did not want me to do, and what I knew myself was not right. Then, at the last minute, I found out something—something I was not meant to know. Found out that a *trap* had been set for me—that my own—that some one very close to me, who should protect me, had given out ideas of evil against me, so that he could say— No, I cannot explain, Father. I feel too shamed.

"I did not know where to go. I can never go home again. I ran back to Mrs. Allen's. And when they saw how I was, Sister Sylvia put her arms around me and said she would be my mother and take me away with her. Oh, she was good to me, Father. So good to me!

"So I am leaving with her on the afternoon train, instead of having gone the other way, on the train last night.

"But, Father, she cannot take me out of the country without permission. Will you see that it is sent to me—New York, this address enclosed? This must be done, Father—even though it might have to be told an evil influence is working against me, and that my home is not a place where I am safe.

"I want to give my life to Jesus. Will you help me, Father? And with money, too? Can you? And soon I will pay you back.

"I hate to go away and leave you. Father, there are things I can't talk about, but I want to say a girl never had a better father. I want to say, a girl never loved her father more. I love you more than any one in the world. Will you remember that, Father—always?

"Your own daughter,
Brook."

BOOK FOUR

CHAPTER XXX

EVANS LEONARD came into that quiet café near the Gare du Nord (the quiet little café because it was the least noisy) where he would meet his mother for the three-ten train for Senlis. Not here yet—after all her warnings to him. Mother was having people out for tea, so they must make this train, Marie might not have seen about the little cakes and things.

The waiter wiped the table and Evans put down the book he had bought over on the Left Bank. "Intimations." He liked the word intimations, rather like a detective story, but on the trail of things you thought by yourself. He opened the book—curious, for what would the intimations be from America? One thought of America as saying it flat, yet here were intimations from a fellow little older than he— this poet was twenty-two, but he himself was going on eighteen. He and Mother would go to America soon now, to see Grandfather Evans. Not that he especially cared about visiting this very old man he had never seen, but it would take him to America, and then he wanted to stay there and go to college.

So what did fellows not much older than he write about in America?

Why did the waiter keep on wiping the table? Oh, yes; this table was here for a drink, not just a book.

Grenadine? Sweet and tiresome. One of the menthes? Vermouth? He was tired of all those French drinks, tired of seeing them around and hearing their names in stuffy places. "Ginger-ale," he said, decisively. Then, *"Attendez!"* He would order something for Mother, who would be almost an hour on the train, after shopping all day. Yes, Mother would like a drink, she wasn't one of the women who could easily order one when alone. "I've had a lot of prissiness wished on me," she would laugh. "The missionaries, your English grandmother—not forgetting my own youth." *"Et vermouth au seltz,"* he added. *"Bien! Bien!"* cried the waiter; a French waiter was always so pleased when he thought you were expecting a lady. And when the lady came in the waiter would be none the less pleased. It wouldn't occur to a waiter that Brook was Evans' mother. Often he thought of her as Brook, because he liked the name—Brook— the sound moved pleasantly in his thoughts.

"Lingering, as light lingers on the broken tree . . ." caught his eye in turning pages.

Why did it make him think of his father? Not two years ago it was—the light falling upon that bed around which they had sat—oh, as long as he could remember. Father calling him in. "Take your mother for a drive, Evans. She simply must get out of this house." It was that morning Mother had pulled out gray hairs, and cried. And when they came back the light had left the bed, and life had left the bed, and Evans suspected what later he came to know, and what his mother did not know, and must never suspect. No, Captain Leonard had died after a long illness—wounds received in the war. Mother's gray hairs had nothing to do with it—nothing. The wonder was her hair wasn't all gray—those nine years of standing by.

This he thought stoutly, for the other thought was trying to break in—that the gray hairs had not multiplied, after all. Mother's beautiful brown hair—gold in it—thick, wavy, yet close-lying, giving that handsome form of her head. He let his thought linger on it with pleasure, pleasure just a little resolute, closing over the thought that it hadn't gone on turning gray, that she needn't have cried. Frowning against what threatened—the wondering, would it have gone on turning gray, if Father hadn't . . . Nonsense! Why *shouldn't* Mother look young? Younger? Younger now than then? Father gone and Mother looking younger? Well, and why not? He faced the ugly thought while reading "Intimations," trying once and for all to tell it to get out, get rid of it. Worry, care, sorrow—rested now..

Mother had wanted the big change, she told him—
leave England, those long hard years, live here in
France—the little house at Senlis. And why not—
he had said then, to himself, to all Father's family.
Certainly she needed this change. It was doing her
good. Sometimes as he saw the beauty sudden color
gave her face, saw how bright—how soft—were her
eyes, Evans did indeed remember a face long seen
upon pillows—no color, no happy expectant light
in eyes, and remembering, the boy suffered, but
suffering—he was glad.

Now Colonel Fowler was coming over to see
them. Father's friend. He had been good to them
all those years. What would they have done without him? Would Mother marry the Colonel?
Why shouldn't she? It seemed the thing to do. It
wouldn't be shutting Father out; they had been together through it all—kind, loyal friend. Turning
the pages of "Intimations," he entertained a few of
his own. One knew a lot one wasn't supposed to
know. What would happen if every one were to
give up what there was between what they were supposed to know and think, and what they really did
know and think? It was from that place, perhaps,
came the "Intimations"—from that place we reached
each other, without ever letting on.

He glanced at his watch, frowned, for he was ac-
customed to responsibilities. Then, looking up, from
the mirror at the back he saw his mother coming

in the door. A moment he continued to look in the mirror, before rising to make himself known.

Yes, the waiter would approve. Evans had never seen his mother look younger. She was excited, there was an eagerness that made her seem young as he. This suit was smart—gray, with suggestions of yellow and of violet—intimations, and now all the women's suits were like school girls'. Mother almost as slim as a girl; she had never put it on. That turban-like hat of very dark red cloth, and the handsome careless scarf. Quick movements as she looked this way and that, her hands a little raised as if helping her in looking, at home anywhere, yet just enough diffident—good style, Mother was.

"Hello," he rescued her. "Have a gulp and we'll dash for the train." He was getting the change from his pocket.

"Dear! We have to go back."

She had sat down, turned toward him, her two hands on the drink which she otherwise disregarded.

"Back where?"

"To the Rue de la Paix."

"Don't be silly. We haven't time."

"We've got to take time. Evans—it's very important."

She was excited, in a curious, a stern sort of way.

"So is it important we get to Senlis to give old lady Maxwell her tea." Yes and it *was* important —these English friends of Grandmother's and

Grandmother not approving of their living in France. Mother couldn't leave people flat like that.

"Darling—listen. There is something I must buy."

There were tears in her excited eyes. She had a glorified look—about something to buy on the Rue de la Paix!

"You can come in and buy it in the morning."

"Oh, no," she said, alarmed. "It might be gone! In fact now—any minute—"

"Listen, Mother. You yourself told me—"

"I know, but that was before I saw it. Come!"

She was hurrying out, and into the taxi she had kept. He could do nothing but get in beside her.

"Is it a dress?" he asked uncordially.

"Yes," she said softly. "It is a dress."

"You said you weren't going to buy any more clothes on those cut-throat streets. You said there was a little place—"

"I know. That was before I saw this one."

"How much does it cost?"

She frowned. "Two thousand francs."

"Oh, *Mother*. And we're borrowing on these securities as it is."

"Yes, the securities. That's why I came for you. We'll not take them out to Senlis—not all of them. I want you to take them over to the bank and tell Mr. Adams— Here, I'll write it."

"I call this taking leave of one's senses!"

"Wait till I show you, and—maybe—tell you."

Held in traffic his mother took out her cigarette case. "Have one?"

"No," said Evans, not making up with her.

"Well, I will," she said, assertively.

But as she smoked her mood changed. "Oh, so strange—here—in Paris—everything so different—so many, many years between."

"I don't understand at all," he said.

"No," his mother replied softly. "In all the world I—only I—understand."

"*Ici!*" she called, rapping.

In this window was one dress. Yellow you would call it, only it was more like light than like any color, unless it were like champagne. A very simple dress—gold underneath, touched here and there with gold thread, one golden rose.

As his mother did not speak or move he turned to her. She was looking straight at the dress, looking through tears.

He took her arm. "Now, Mother, really! It's lovely—yes, but if you are getting it for the Colonel, won't he be in very good spirits about that silver dress?"

"I am not getting it for the Colonel."

"For me, perhaps?" Evans asked ironically.

She shook her head, smiling. "No, dear, not for you."

"For whom then?" he demanded.

"For my mother," she said, and he had never seen her face like this.

But what was one to make of it? Her mother had been dead years and years.

CHAPTER XXXI

BROOK lighted the candles beside the mirror. She had put the dress on without really look-at herself. She had even declined to try it at the shop—"I know it will be all right." She wanted to see herself in it all at once, at the moment.

Indeed she did not look even now, but did a few things about her room, putting away clothes she had taken off. She loved her room in this house on the old ramparts at Senlis, especially she loved it after the candles had been lighted—these red hangings, neither somber nor bright, her desk—she had found it in Avignon, this chair, so comfortable and of such beauty, with dignity expressing the fading loveliness of old France. Marie had made the room ready for the night—reading-lamp on the little table by the bed, slippers, robe.

Before going to bed she would pull the heavy curtains, step out on the balcony and from her high place look across the country to darkness that was the forest of Chantilly. In the morning the sun would come in, she would sit up in bed and, waiting for her coffee, watch the procession of the fields—new wheat against the rich tone of plowed earth;

the huge carts—like a story one would love in child-
hood; horses plowing, sometimes ponderous white
oxen—motors too, trees along the narrow stream.
"Live through the night, Mother?" Evans would
call. "Feeling fit? Going to market?" This
they loved to do, for market was in a fourteenth-
century church, carts wide with carrots moved down
the aisle, women smiling among their cheeses and
fruits.

Other mornings, as they heard the cathedral bell,
"Let's go to church," Evans might propose, and as
they came up the narrow, walled street to the cathedral square, "Why weren't you born a Catholic,
Mother?" he would complain. Suddenly loyal to
the ugly little Protestant church in Santa Clara,
where she had so many Sundays gone with her
father, she might reply, primly: "I am very proud
to have been born a Protestant." He would laugh
at her, her boy who understood so many things it
would not seem his years had had time to teach him
—and she knew he was thinking, though affectionately, that while she might be proud, she never went
to church unless she were in England, and had to go
with the family.

Her life here, though simple, had a completeness
within its own form, a realization of what itself was,
that gave the feel of luxury. Within her garden
wall she walked at evening, as any lady of old France,
and when herself partaking of their pleasures there

went over her, as a blessing, the gentle breath from vanished charm.

She was seated in this chair graciously rounded to her back. She had not yet seen herself in the dress she had been compelled to buy. But her hand was moving upon it. She lifted the long wing that drooped from the shoulder. Oh the lovely stuff —shimmering, as if made with light itself. Seeing her hand beneath it, as if it were there she saw another hand draping another fabric—"silk muslin," that was called, and the hand that touched it moved with care, not alone in feeling, but because so roughened by work it might break the fine threads. "At the neck it should be simple—like you had your chemise pulled down yesterday."

"Mother!"

Brook started. Oh, of course, it was Evans, calling from the stairway. She had been hearing another voice, living in its every intonation, as if the dress had given it life.

As she did not answer, he was at the door.

"There's a carnival over at—"

She had risen and he stood staring at her, leaning back against the door, so startled, overwhelmed, that she laughed.

"Well of all—" he began, but ended in a long, low whistle. "It's a knock-out," he admitted.

"Why, Mother, you look about twenty-three years old!"

Flushed, smiling, she turned to the mirror. She too was startled.

"Oh, you are lovely, Mother," her boy cried. ("Oh, you are lovely, darling!" she heard the other voice, the voice she had not heard for twenty years.)

She was indeed more beautiful now than when her mother helped her dress for the dance with Tony. Strange she could look young, after all there had been. Short hair was good for her, for her head had nice form. Mother was right—the gold of the dress brought golden light to her eyes, and found the gold of her hair. She had not had to touch it up. Very few gray hairs, after all. She shouldn't have let Bert hear her cry, that day she pulled them out. She had not known she was going to cry. It had all at once come, as if something in her had broken down. But she had cried very little, she hastened to think—very little, through the nine years.

"But where'll you wear it?" Evans was asking.

"Oh, I'll wear it to-morrow night. Dinner in Paris—at the Burtons'."

"With the Colonel?"

"With the Colonel." And regarding herself she had to laugh. Shoulders and throat rose from a golden cloud. Her arms were lovely under this spun light, beautiful as they emerged. One of those dresses for which one wore little underneath—so slim a dress, and grave middle age at the Burtons'.

But afterwards they might go to Hélène's. Who
could tell—the dress made her think—what might
not happen?

"All right, dear," she said to Evans, who would
join the Edwards boys, going over on bicycles to a
street fair at Armenonville.

He came running back with a letter that had come
for her in the last post. "American," he said.
"From Illinois."

"It's Uncle Willie's writing. It must be about
Father."

Outside his friends summoned and Evans called,
"Good-by!"

Brook was a little fearful of opening the letter.
She had been meaning to go home and see her father.
She had never seen him since she said good-night to
him when he would leave early next morning for the
mountains. The war—then all those years Bert was
helpless. She could not leave; since then she had
been—reorganizing things. She was meaning to
go now, very soon. After her father became too
old to be alone in Colorado he went back where he
used to live. In fact, he lived now at the Kellogg
place, Uncle Willie taking care of him, because the
house belonged in part to his sister Naomi. "And
Father said," Uncle Willie wrote Brook, telling her
they would take Caleb in, "that if ever we could do
anything for Caleb, we were to do it, because he had
once done a great thing for our family. Father was

dying when he said this, so I've no idea what he meant, but I remember his words and shall act according."

After delaying a while, trying her hair straight back, a bit of make-up, Brook turned from herself to her letter.

"Dear Brook," wrote this uncle whom she had never seen. "You talked about coming home to see your father, bringing Evans. Well, I'm not much of a hand to write, but seems like I ought to tell you if you want to see him, better not wait too long. You know he's more than seventy now and seems like in the last month he's grown older even than that. 'Twas hard for him to get upstairs, so we gave him the downstairs bedroom—the same as used to be Naomi's. He talks about you. 'Brook is coming to see me,' he says. 'And my grandson. My grandson is named Evans,'—that's what he keeps telling everybody. Seems like it would be too bad if he was to slip away in his sleep, never seeing his only grandson, when the boy seems to be so much on his mind. So I thought maybe I ought to let you know how things are, for I know you've always set great store by your father and been good to him. Guess he won't hold out much longer—leastwise not in his mind. They get childish, you know.

"Well, Brook, seems like there's not much news to tell you, when you're so far away, and we not acquainted, except by letter. Rosie's folks are pretty well, though her girl lost this last baby. This old place is lively—Frank still here and Grace came back home after her husband died. Her two young-ones are a handful. Guess I told you the youngest is named Naomi. Seems natural to be hearing it, though truth to tell I don't much remember my sister Naomi, being only seven when she left.

"Our Frank's got a good job in a garage now; goes back and forth in his own Chevrolet. The town's building out this way so fast seems we won't be country much longer. Got a chance to sell some of the land, and maybe we will. I'll be getting old to farm it, and none of my boys or Rosie's wants to work it. Machinery, that's where the money is now, they say. This would be land the brook is on, and I believe they aim to take the brook, higher up, for concrete work. We'd miss it, for we always had it, but progress is progress. It's the brook you were named for, so better come back whilst you can still hear it, and before your father is too far away in his mind.

"I've had a cold, but it's better. Excuse mistakes, but the radio is making such a noise. Frank made it himself, and we get Chicago.

"Your Uncle Willie."

She would have to go. She should have gone be-fore now—but Evans' school, one thing and another. How very old her father would be, for he had always seemed old. To-morrow they would go to Paris and see about sailings. It would be expensive—but what a horrid thing to consider, when her father had been so good to her, sending her money after she left home, though he had so little himself. Perhaps he had had to mortgage the place; she had suspected it, but had not wanted to know.

Yes, how good he had always been to her! She must take Evans to see him, before he got "too far away in his mind."

The relatives would be rather dreadful. How would Evans get on with them—after England, where his life had been so different? But he would be a good sort, for he was that. How proud his grandfather would be of him! The boy had poise—distinction. They said he looked like his father's people. But she knew that his eyes were her mother's eyes.

She must write her father to-night—yes and she would cable, letting him have the pleasure of anticipation. And then she would have to go. That would settle it for her. If anything happened—no, she would never forgive herself. They would not need to be there long. And when she came back?

Oh, yes, she conceded, with a somewhat weary impatience, when she came back she would marry Colonel Fowler. It was expected of her. It seemed the thing to do. He had been so good to Bert, to them all, through those years. Bert would want her to do it, feeling that she would be cared for, that his old friend, his colonel, would look after his boy. Oh, he would look after him, she thought, wryly. She and Evans would become the regiment. The instinct to organize, benevolently command, would organize their walks. "You go forward three kilometres on the highway, after which you take the first turning to the left. You will have lunch at the inn behind the stone wall. You must not let them give you soup, for you cannot rely upon the meat. But you may have an omelet." When they came home they must make their report, and he was so pleased, affectionately approving, when all had gone as arranged, and they would, in spite of themselves, find themselves apologetic, trying to be ingratiating, if they had deviated from orders.

He had not approved of her taking this house in France. "Certainly you will want to come to Paris from time to time," he said, indulgently, for he was a reasonably indulgent officer, "but your home should be in England." "Why should it?" she asked herself, but did not ask him, for that one did not much do, and for years she had let him tell her what to do about Bert. Oh, how kind he had been, she thought, warmer to him. And he would be kind, very kindly indeed would direct her, arranging her life.

When he asked her to marry him she had said, "Can't we talk about that a little later?" He had accepted her feeling, for Bert had been dead little

more than a year then. But to-morrow he was ar-
riving in Paris, and she knew why.

Say Yes now, perhaps, and be married as soon as
she came back from America. That would put it
off a little longer. Though why should she wish to
put it off? It really wasn't quite nice of her—their
dear old friend. What else did she expect? What
was there to expect? The youthful feeling the dress
had given her was as something running down. Why
did this thought of marrying the Colonel make her
feel so much older? People would say she was a
very fortunate woman; as indeed she was, she agreed
stoutly. Nothing to be deplored in a woman only
two years from forty marrying a man of fifty-four.
Thirty-eight. One's youth is gone at thirty-eight.
She ran her hands through her thick short hair. Of
course one's youth was gone at thirty-eight, and she
was not going to be one of those silly women, running around alone, trying to seem younger than
she was. Like Hélène. It was undignified, and she
had never been undignified. She had a feeling she
must marry Colonel Fowler because it would be undignified not to. Of course England had been dreary
for her before, because Bert was ill. It would be
different now. A good home, enough money—good,
though sober, connections. A woman "getting on,"
not much money, a son to think of, what more could
she ask?

She went to the dressing-table to run the comb

through the hair she had deranged in asking herself, not once, but again and again, what more one
could ask. Rowdyish this way, and amused her;
she shook her head, letting it go here and there, and
looking like a little girl. Laughing at herself it was
suddenly as if she met those very blue eyes—strong,
laughing eyes of the crazy Icelander, as they called
him at Hélène's, Erik Helge, the mad mathematician.
Now why should she think of *him?* Perhaps because he was always running his hands through his
thick red hair, tossing his head, as he put life in
terms of mathematics, and somehow, even for an ignorant person like Brook, made the mathematics
sing. A violent, electric person. Fire of the frosty
north. Yes, of course he would be let out from
college—a dangerous teacher. Elasticity of youth—
though really, judging by all he had done, he must
be about forty himself—one of the men who did not
seem it. His eyes the other night as he combated
—indeed demolished—Hélène's friend from the
Sorbonne—sparks from thought seemed given off
from them. Throwing her head back, again tossing
her hair, she felt as if she were dancing with him.
This dress would be nice for dancing! Suddenly, for
no reason she could have given, she thought of her
mother.

Gray calico she wore—moving from room to room
in that gaunt, lonely house. "This is for you, darling"—a tender voice, but always anxious. Lonely

—hours and hours all alone. Still by the mirror, hair not made orderly, still flushed by that feeling of dancing with the strong Northerner, charged with what thought of him had brought, she met the life in her own eyes, saw the thought in them before she quite knew she was thinking it—that she was as old now as her mother had been when last she saw her. This woman at whom she looked, in the dress her mother had wanted for her, radiant, eager in the thought of dancing with that man all life, she—Brook—was as old now as the woman who stood by the side of the house extending her arms to the daughter who left her alone.

"I must write to Father," Brook thought, not the courage to go on thinking of her mother. For what could she do now—that lonely figure so far in the past? She went to her desk. "Dear Father," she began, but after a little found she was making aimless marks on the paper. She crumpled it and took another. "Dear—" She sat looking down at it. "Mother," something within her said. It rose, took her, "Mother!"

CHAPTER XXXII

HER mother had lived for eight years after she left her alone on the prairie that day. "You must write to your mother," her father would urge. "Maybe it will rouse her." She would send letters about what she was doing. Her mother would not reply. "Seems like she can't write," her father would say. "Seems like she moves in a daze." "After I told her," he wrote Brook, in asking her to write to her mother, "that night I came back and told her, she ran out of the house. I couldn't find her. Not till morning did she come back. Since then, seems like she moves in a daze."

"Perhaps Mother would like to go back home," she wrote her father, after she had married, and had a little money. "No," he replied, "she doesn't want to go back home."

One day in England, Bert fighting in France, she and Evans living with his mother, she took from the hall table a letter from her father. She went in the garden to read it. "Dear Brook," he wrote, "It's sad news I have to write this time. Yesterday morning I woke and said to your mother, 'Must be time to get up.' Ever since you went away we've slept side by side." (Strange he should say that—just then.) "She didn't answer. Asleep, I thought; I'll not wake her. But as I was getting dressed, it struck me funny. She was dead.

"Seems like she looks more herself than she has for years. I'm taking her back home to be buried, by her folks and near her—well, her old friends, you might say. Seems like that's the right thing to do, though she never got over the mountains herself. I wish you was here. We been together a long time—" (The writing was broken.) "Seems lonely—lost like—without Naomi.

"Your Father."

She had thought her mother would be glad when she married, and wrote her a long letter about that. "Guess your mother is sure glad you are happy," her father replied, "but she don't say much these days." And then about Evans. "Well, I wish I could see my grandson," he wrote. "And maybe I will some day—maybe we will. I guess you know your mother is glad you have a baby, but she's no hand to write these days."

And what had she thought about, those seven years—"no hand to write"; moving as in a daze? Was it indeed a daze—dulling loneliness, heartbreak?

Heartbreak, yes. "I broke her heart," Brook said, sitting very still before her desk, facing it as she had never faced it, wanting now to know, not so much either to vindicate or to blame herself, as somehow, though too late, to clear a place between her and her mother, wanting understanding to be there, if only for its own sake, and so at last asking, searching.

Why had there not been ease between her and her mother? From the very first, as far back as she could remember, she had known that here was a love that would do anything in the world for her—die for her, suffer, do wrong for her. She had soon come to know that her mother did not exist for herself, but existed for Brook. Why should this, of all things, exasperate one? Why was it so hard for her to show love in response to the completeness of this love? In any kind of emotional moment why would she be constrained, awkward, and finally resentful?

Not so much in the first days, when she accepted her mother as the one to care for her. Alone there together when Brook was a child there was companionship. Yes, her mother must have had happiness in her then, she thought, now that she could never make her happy again. "Mamma!" she could hear herself calling. "Yes, darling." They played games together, there alone on the prairie.

There was a tensity in her mother's love. Was that what irked her? Did she resent the knowledge it was she alone her mother loved—as if this were a responsibility, making her the other part of something not of her choosing? Did she feel herself surrounded with love from too lonely an intensity, and was that why she liked the easier give-and-take with her father and other people? She wanted to know. Merely to condemn herself was too easy. On the surface of it anybody would condemn her. But there must be something underneath, and into that she pried and pushed her way to-night. She was not more cold-hearted, selfish, than most people. She was not a monster. She had disliked herself for coldness and was not happy in things she did. But that was no answer. Why? Why had there never been loving ease between her and the lonely woman who would have suffered anything in the world to make it better for her?

Once or twice, when first she knew Tony, she had almost gone out to her mother, happy that she could. And then it would give her an awkward, foolish, and finally that resentful feeling. This was something she did not want her mother to touch, not wanting to share with her, as if something in herself were aware of things she did not yet know. No, that was fantastic; but her mother's experience—that early tragedy, long bitter loneliness, love that never died, made her something from which Brook held back. And finally Mother should not have told it as she did—her own story, not just then.

Girls were different now. The world seemed to

have become a different place, though, to be sure, she now touched a world far from those early days. Were there daughters now who were at ease with their mothers? Was hers, even then, a very particular case? The church—Sylvia Waite—that was the world she knew; that was "right." Yet Mother did not accept it as the world, as right. Would Mother, in any case, have been different? That she would like to know. For some reason, that she would very much like to know.

It was not alone the world immediately around her made her mother's love story thus tend to turn her from love. It was something within herself— as something left there—a resistance, a stubbornness. Of the people behind her, it was only her mother she knew. Her Grandfather and Grandmother Kellogg, Brook believed she would have felt at home with them. And there was some one else—named Joe. Yes, her father. Really, her own father. Even yet it was hard to think this; she thought it furtively, for *Father* was her father, all her loyalty, her stubbornness from the past, made him that. Yet, as a matter of fact, she was this other man's child. What was he like? She did not really know at all. A lover—her mother said, and even now the word brought distaste. His eyes—his smile— she saw her mother as she talked of them, then tried not to see her . . .

No, she did not know what he was, nor what the

people behind him were, except that his mother must have been very strict, and had been cruel to Mother. And then Brook had been cruel to Mother—as if going on with something.

Oh, no, she thought, impatiently pushing back her hair—no, that was not it, surely not. But when one is in love for the first time, when a girl has been much by herself, there is something about love she does not want any one else to—lay a hand on. It wasn't only that her mother made her fiercely loyal to her father; it was that she was not willing to share love with her mother, especially after she knew. What she was feeling then became as what her mother had felt. No! something in her said— something outraged, afraid, proud, stubborn, superior. Something pretty hard and small, it seemed now. For some reason she had wanted to punish, defeat her mother, even though it took her own love. It was strange—a sorry thing to think about, and thinking of it did not let her understand.

Those last days she had to resist a suspicion her mother knew she was meeting Tony, would not let herself really encounter the suspicion. She had so strongly taken the stand for her father, and the things her mother had said about love made her feel—something like naked. She could not go ahead if she went as one with her mother. So she left her out, though taking all she could get from her! "A little hypocrite, that's what I was," said the woman who considered it to-night. "A self-righteous, heartless prig. A sneaky prude." Yet calling herself those names, even meaning them, did not throw upon it the light of understanding. To blame was not enough; that did not clear the place between her and her mother which it seemed understanding might clear, even now.

She had not wanted to be what she was being. Those last days were almost unbearable. What was it kept her from doing what she would have been happier to do, say to her mother, "I find I love Tony, and now I am going to marry him, even against Father's wishes." Knowing her mother had so little, why did she have to deny her the happiness of that confidence, the pleasure of openly doing together those last things, instead of forcing her mother to do them in lonely estrangement? How she would have loved to talk of what Brook's life would be. How brave she would have been about it all. Oh, indeed how brave, how deeply loving and un-self-seeking she had been!

Tears now.

There had been tears then—a few, as she kissed her mother good-by. She was glad to remember them—meager feeling though they were. There was a moment when she wanted to say, "Mother, you understand, don't you?" But she had not said it, and the mother who was to be left there alone, knowing, gave no sign. How could Mother have done it, loving as she did? It was great, Brook said in tardy tribute, it was great! Almost she had run back; seeing her mother standing there alone she had almost run back in horror, for she knew to what it was she left her. "But Mother wants me to go," she told herself, and did no more than turn again, throwing a kiss. At that her mother's arms extended—reached—reaching far as they could toward the child—child she had never reached. Brook's arms went as to reach out now, across more than the prairie, but she covered her face, trying to shut out this picture of the brave lonely mother she never saw again.

But when Tony told her—how stupid of him to have told her—then her whole feeling turned in one angry tide against her mother. She did not even love Tony any more, all her emotion going to the fury that she had been thus betrayed—that all the while her mother had been knowing, had arranged it, telling him those shameful things about her birth, giving him the idea . . . Even after all these years her face burned in the memory of what she had felt then.

They were walking along the lane, under the birches; Brook was much shaken by her good-by to her mother, to Sylvia Waite, that she would not see her father again, deceiving him, deeply disappointing. Tony was comforting her, as they waited for the stage. They would be married at the Junction, he said. But she was frightened, leaving these streets she knew, leaving every one she knew and in this secret way going into an unknown world. She was deceiving her father, she said, and he soothed her, saying that couldn't be helped, and her father would forgive her when he saw she was happy. And how cruel she had been, needlessly deceiving her mother, she kept saying, until Tony assured her, "Don't worry about that. Your mother knows. It is what she wants." Then she got it from him, though he tried to deny part of it. But when she knew her mother had dared tell him Father was not her father—"I will not be tricked! I will not be trapped like this!"—broke from him, ran fast as she could toward home, then knew she could not go home— stopping at the Allens' and almost beside herself pouring out her story to Sylvia Waite—how her mother did not want her to be good, how she was plotting against her. "Dear child!" Sister Sylvia would comfort. "There—there! You were right to come to me. I will guard you. God will protect you, dear child." And Mrs. Allen saying, "We have feared for some time your mother was not quite —steady in her mind. Of course you cannot be with her, if she has this idea against you." And they counseled together, how Brother Evans would want them to take the responsibility. Now that there was danger at home he would not want Brook to lose this opportunity to go with Sylvia, join with her in doing God's work, and there find salvation. "I will take the responsibility," Mrs. Allen said, and Brook agreed, for she must get away, and she knew that nothing could hurt her mother more than this.

CHAPTER XXXIII

SHE had soon come to dislike Sister Sylvia's voice. It was monotonously bright and strong. Even while her heart was still hard against her mother she knew her mother had a beautiful voice—would know it when Sylvia's left her in this boredom. Yet things were interesting at first. She liked the trip, the romantic feeling of being so far away; so much in feeling having been cut off, there was real fervor for "the work."

The second year Sylvia was transferred to Smyrna. It was there Brook met Bert. Brook had no appointment as a missionary, she was a helper, a student. It was important she make part of her own money, so in the afternoon she taught the children of an English family. One day she saw a young officer there. "Who is the beautiful girl?" she heard him ask Mrs. Dwight, as she passed through the hall. The next day Mrs. Dwight introduced them, and he would walk home with her.

Sylvia did not discourage this. "It may be," she said, "that you are not called to the work." Brook was not unaware of being something of an embarrassment to them, as her position was not official.

"You can do God's work wherever you are," Sylvia said. "You must not feel you have to stay among us." For they all saw that the handsome lieutenant was in love with "the missionary girl." Bert was not the sort of officer Sylvia would distrust. "Of course his ideas are not ours," she said. "He is of the world. But he is a Christian, and a gentleman. I believe he is a good man."

So Brook said Yes, and they were married at the mission.

In a short time Bert was ordered to Constantinople.

Life was different there—gay, and indeed worldly. Sometimes dressing for dinner, perhaps an Embassy dance, Brook would feel a little dazed by the swift changes in her life. It was here she met Hélène, the popular young Madame Verpont, who shocked and fascinated her. "Why, the blessed lamb!" Hélène would cry, if Brook turned from a story; or, "Now, that's Mamma's dear good little girl!" when Brook unsympathetically received account of how long the party had gone on, what happened. "Was her sweet innocent child from America? Did her never let naughty man kiss her?" Hélène would tease. Hélène was good for her, she decided, thinking of this friendship in thinking of all things to-night.

Yet she and Bert were not of Hélène's gayest world. Sylvia had seen him pretty well. He was not like the missionaries, yet he was apart from that mad crowd in Constantinople, would not have wanted her to be of it. "I wish I were brilliant, like Hélène," she had said, and he pushed back her hair, holding her face in his hands as he murmured: "How I love you for your differences from Hélène!" "You are so good, darling," he would say—and once laughed, "Why, you are as good as if you were not beautiful!" He would tease her about the fidelity with which she kept up missionary work in gay Constantinople. "But I love you for it," he would assure, and once, "It is a joke that stern old church-goers should go right on living in you." Though he was a great one to talk, in him, too, lived the more rigorous things behind him.

She loved Bert, but not with mad gayety, or with mad passion. They might have been a good deal older than they were . . .

Very soon she knew she was going to have a baby. And not long after Evans was born—the war.

Months—years, of waiting in England. And then, almost at the close of the war, Bert wounded. Years of illness.

So life had not been as gay for her as some of its moments promised. In feeling, she was still not far from the Brook Evans of Santa Clara, Colorado. As if there were much that she would some time know, but did not know yet. As if there were that which waited.

"Mother!"

Evans back! All evening she had sat looking into things, looking, and not seeing as she wanted to see, seeing but a little. Was that past irrevocable? If it would not give up its secrets to her, then it was indeed irrevocable.

"Come in, dear."

He started to tell her of his evening, but she put her hands on his shoulders, searching his face.

"What is it?" he asked.

"I want to see—whom you look like."

"This the first chance you've had?" he laughed.

"In the obvious things—your father's people. But all around the eyes, the way it is formed—the look in the eyes—sometimes the mouth—yes, she is there! And the voice. Sometimes that voice speaks again."

"Well, Mother—any time you are ready to tell me what you are talking about—"

"Was the carnival fun?"

"Lost thirty francs. But won these shooting." He produced cigar-holder and pepper-shaker. But as he was telling her of the "shoot the shoots" she said: "We must go to America at once. If I let my father die, never having seen him again! Oh, I have enough to be sorry for, without that."

"I don't think you have much to be sorry for."

"Yes, dear; I have."

He turned from her. "Not about Father."

"About Father, perhaps not."

Yes, she had been good to Bert. Her days had been given to him, through years. It would be too shameful to fail in all one's relationships, so she was glad to remember that Bert would tell her—happily, gratefully, sadly, she was good to him. "But it wasn't what I had meant to take you into," he would say, holding her hand, looking into her face, more pain in his eyes than pain brought there. "You know, Brook darling," he had smiled at her, "I thought of myself as rescuing you."

"From the missionaries?"

"Yes, the missionaries. And from your own goodness. A certain kind of goodness that was too hard on you, took too much. Almost before I loved you I felt you must be rescued. You were for something else. You were for life. But I had not meant —sitting by a sick man's bed."

And she would talk warmly of happy times they had had. "And will again," she would say, even able to look at him, smiling, as she said it, though she did not believe it would again be more than this. And sometimes—oh, glad to remember, after to-night's bitter memories—tenderness, feeling for him would melt that which kept her from another, and with something as near abandonment as she had known in her life she could caress, kneel, or lie by him, kiss him as she said: "Suppose you had not come back at all! Suppose I did not have you!" He would hold her head tight against him, and she could feel emotion flowing through his hands. In some of these moments of his sickness they were closer than in the closest moments of his strength.

But those were the rare times. As the years went on her goodness was a little like the old fervor in "doing good." Did she become the missionary again, after all? And then when she saw that her hair was turning gray in this service, suddenly that Brook who had been rescued—who had had something of life, and suspected, half unsuspectingly, there was much she had never had—tears had come, sobs, for the years that were going by.

"But I should not have cried over my gray hair." She said it to Evans, though a little ashamed of herself, again asking reassurance from her boy.

He had turned to her dressing-table, his back to her—was screwing and unscrewing the top of her cold-cream jar. "Isn't it about time for you to stop thinking of that? It didn't—mean anything, and you know it." He said it quietly, rather as if bored. But in the mirror she saw his profile, face lowered.

He looked tired, pale, not youthful in this moment. Had riding on that silly thing at the carnival made him a little ill?

"The trip to America will do you good," she said. "We won't be on one of the fastest boats, they are too expensive. It will be nice to have all those days on the ocean."

"What about the Colonel?"

"The Colonel?"

"Isn't he coming to-morrow?"

"Yes."

"Isn't he coming to see you?"

"To see us, among other things. But we'll have a week or so before our sailing."

"Maybe he'd like to go with us," Evans laughed.

"Oh, no."

"Going to marry him, Mother?"

For her son to ask this, it made her heart beat; she felt the blood rising to her face. "What do you think about it?" she laughed.

"Me? What have I to say about it?"

"A good deal," she answered.

What was he feeling? Something of resentment, pain, because of his father? His face looked as if this might be, but what he said was, fingering the gaudy cigar-holder he had again picked up: "I think Father would be glad."

"Yes," she agreed, and felt suddenly as if something were settled, and felt in her spirit as one may feel when the color goes out of the western sky.

"Oh, that is if you want to," said Evans, as if irritated by the embarrassment in which he found himself. "What do I know about it?" He yawned. "I'm sleepy," and he got away more quickly than he usually said good-night.

Standing by the mirror, getting ready to go to bed, this seemed an absurd dress for her to have. It was

too young for her. And what was there to *do* with
it?

The window open, she lay looking through the
trees, across the wide stretch between her and the
forest. At home she used to lie looking across the
valley to Big Chief. Marriage, pleasures of the
world, some happiness, a baby, years of anxiety—
death, and with it all she did not feel much older or
unlike that girl who would look across the valley to
the mountains that shut one from the East. She
could see herself coming along home from school,
and she might have gone that road yesterday, might
be setting out upon it again to-morrow. Sometimes
it was like that, sometimes those years were another
life, another world. She had been much loved. Her
mother, her father, her husband, her son. She had
had the love of men—Tony, Bert—dear Bert, so
good to her; now Andrew, Colonel Fowler. But
what did her mother *mean?* Just what did her
mother mean—those things she said about love?
Was there something she—Brook—did not know?
Was she incapable of knowing? There had been
nothing in her own life that would have gone on
living through twenty barren years. Mother had
known only a few months of love—then loss, shame,
and—oh, loneliness—long, relentless. But there was
a light that never went out. It burned in tragic
beauty until—until I put out all light of her spirit,
thought Brook. But she—Brook—was the child of

that love. There were secrets she did not know.
Mathematics. Not just a dull book one figured in
the Santa Clara high school. A rhythm, an undis-
covered country. Secrets that could sing. Iceland.
Long lonely twilights in the North. Then winters
that were dark. Yes, winter—dark winter. And
death—dark, lonely. But a long strange twilight.
"Oh, you are lovely, darling!" her mother had said.
Was that just to-night? No, it was Evans had said
it to-night—"Oh, you are lovely, Mother!" Life
was confused. Perhaps not if you understood it.
So she was going to marry Andrew, Colonel Fowler.
It was settled. Was it? There is a light from blue
eyes fighting with thought like—like sunlight on a
glacier.

CHAPTER XXXIV

A YOUNG French composer was playing his "new music" at Hélène's that night. "Oh, I am so glad you are here, Colonel Fowler," their hostess greeted them, as Brook and the Colonel arrived with the Burtons and a few others with whom they had been dining. "We are going to drive you quite mad," she went on in her lively fashion, "and it will be delightful to observe." The Colonel smiled securely—any one who wished to observe him being driven quite mad by any young man's music was welcome to the spectacle, he seemed to say. "Such music is very good for the English," Hélène told him. "I am sure it cannot do them a bit of harm," the Colonel replied. "But, my *dear!*" she exclaimed, looking Brook up and down and turning her around. "If you *can* look like this—why have you never done so before?"

"I did once," said Brook. "Once before. You like it?" she asked, for she had been uncertain of her dress with the others. Colonel Fowler had said, "So that is why you like to live in France!" But she surmised he was a little disconcerted by his admiration; and Mrs. Burton, no older than Brook, wore discreetly fashioned gray.

"It is just the dress for one who has a missionary taint," said Hélène. "There might be worse taints," Brook did not neglect to affirm.

The music amused and excited Brook. Yes, one could do that with music. Why not?

"Do you like it?" she asked the Colonel.

"No," he replied. "I am very fond of music." And she heard him telling Mrs. Burton, of course one could do that if one wanted to—any one could —just as one could read Shakespeare by pulling the words all out of order, shrieking and bellowing some, moaning and hissing others. But just what would be the advantage, he wanted to know. "One has to think of it as—like the Russian," Mrs. Burton said uncertainly. The Colonel thought it bad enough to have the Russian without having to think of something as like it.

"Music should be orderly," said Brook, a little maliciously.

"Exactly," he said firmly.

The next piece was even less orderly—unless it might have an order of its own. It held her in a curious way, for it, too, seemed a search for a secret. It was like things that had been going on in her mind. It was disturbing, yet somehow just outside what you would like to have disturbed, as if it had moved over somewhere else, just a little way, but enough to make all the difference. She was not sure it should have done that. At least she was not sure

she could connect with it. Turning her head in
thinking of it, trying to follow, wishing to be something more than excited, she saw that Erik Helge was
standing by the door. One hand was in his thick
red hair, his eyes looking, not at the musicians, but
ahead—not excited, but alert—following, understanding, as if he were in the midst of something he
was pushing through. Then his eyes moved and he
saw Brook. She did not nod, nor did she at once
look away, as for the moment he looked straight at
her, not seeing her, his eyes still charged with hard
thinking going on in him. They had that look of
fire and frost—not his violent look now, but concen-
trated, intensively alive.

But after he had been looking at her a moment
he saw her, and she felt the blood coming to her
face—she still blushed, as when a girl; all of that
concentration seemed turned upon her, and the
quality of it began to change: something of wonder,
made her flush the more and lower her eyes. The
pleasure—yes, a sort of bald astonishment that
music was heightening—more swift and discordant,
going from that into a very high, thin element—
tenuous and increasingly excited; and as it—one
might say screeched, only, it seemed, searched, into
some farthest place, without knowing she was going
to do so she raised her eyes and found those ardent
frosty blue eyes had not left her face. They held
her own eyes, and the moment had an intimacy un-

like any she had ever known, so that at last she must break it with a conventional nod; but he refused thus to break it and she turned a little away knowing those eyes—bluer, more direct, more vital than she had even seen them—would not leave her face.

"It doesn't seem respectable," Mrs. Burton murmured.

Brook started. Oh—she meant the music.

Later she talked with the composer. As she turned back to her own party Erik Helge stepped up to her. "Let's go somewhere and dance," he said.

What an idea! *She* leave here, leave the people she came with—leave the Colonel!—and go running off alone to dance with Erik Helge? "Oh, I can't," she said, and felt she sounded very young and foolish.

"What's to stop you?" He took her arm and directed her away from the others. "We'll get right away, before any one knows!"

"I am with Colonel Fowler," said Brook with dignity.

"Fowler—who's he?"

"Well, what's the difference who he is?" Brook laughed.

"The elderly Englishman who sat by you?"

"Elderly! What do you mean—elderly?" But it seemed she had let herself get very intimate with him, thus quarreling. Why did she not manage it with some poise? "Thank you very much," she said, like the prim Brook Evans of old, "but it is not possible."

"Anything is possible," he told her. "Anything. Oh, lots harder things than this." His hand on her arm, she could do nothing but move still farther from the others. "You see this door? Then through a hall into another door. There you have a cloak—I suppose you have. Then a taxi to Ciro's. If it's crowded we'll go to the Bois. I want to dance with you. I want to talk with you. To-night I saw you—as if I had not seen before. I had known that you were beautiful, but it did not seem to matter, not especially. Now it matters. Brook—your name is Brook, isn't it?—before that seemed a little foolish. Now it means something. Brook. Yes—Brook. But we can talk better after we have danced. Come! Suppose something happened—and we never saw each other again!"

Oh, yes—quite mad. Who was mad? She must be, for she heard herself saying: "First I must speak to my friends."

Yes, suddenly quite mad, and with all the craft of it, for she found herself saying to the Colonel: "I am sorry, but I am running along now. Something —arranged before I knew you were coming. But you are coming out to-morrow, to stay several days with us? It is nice to feel you are here"—said it as she would not have believed she could have said it to the Colonel, leaving him quite unequal to a reply.

Not so Hélène, who had seen, and came into the hall as they joined each other with their wraps.

"Leaving?" she asked, in assumed astonishment.

"I didn't want to interrupt you to say good-night," said Brook. "I was going to telephone you in the morning."

"Were you really?" replied Hélène; and Brook saw that she was displeased. Hélène was jealous of her! Though she was beautiful, women had not been jealous of Brook.

"The music was interesting," said Erik. "A little—a little too exact. One misses the old chaos, sentimental though they made it. But it was nice to hear. Now we must run along and dance."

Brook was annoyed. Why need he have said it? Perhaps he knew Hélène would suspect.

"Well, Brook," cried Hélène, in her old manner, but not the old friendliness underneath, "if you are running along to dance with Erik—watch your step!"

"Oh, I am a good dancer," said Erik blandly.

"Yes. Just the dancer for a missionary girl."

"Who's a missionary girl? Are you a missionary girl?" he demanded of Brook, with amused zest. "I knew we had a lot to talk about!" he cried, impatiently, as if being held from what he wanted.

"Dear—dear!" mocked Hélène. "Don't let me —detain you, for one instant!"

Brook, smiling, put out a hand that would ingratiate; but, "What am I to do with your Colonel Fowler?" Hélène asked, not agreeably.

"Oh, the English always know what to do with themselves," Erik assured her. "Good-night, Hélène."

Outside the door Brook hesitated. "I feel I have been rude. Hélène does not like our going."

He laughed. "You think Hélène would not go— if she wanted to—and had the chance?"

If she had the chance! To-night it was Brook who had the chance, leaving Hélène angry. She should be sorry, anxious, too—for what might Hélène not say to the Colonel? But she was too excited to consider this now.

CHAPTER XXXV

THERE was something she should be thinking of. "I must get that last train!" she exclaimed.

"Train? Where?"

"To Senlis. Where I live." Suppose Evans knew she had not come home, and was worried!

"This is too good a one to miss," he tempted her, and they were dancing again. "After this one," she said firmly.

Curious their dancing should make them so acquainted. She had loved dancing, and she had not had a great deal of it. There had been something impersonal in it for her—a good dancer was a good dancer. Not since that one dance she went to with Tony, so long ago, had the excitement, the happiness, been because of the man with whom she danced. As Erik held her—not too closely, not with importunity, her whole consciousness was that they did this together. She was in the rhythm of him, charged with that electric thing she had felt from him even before she had been close to him; now she was close to him, and felt that for him, too, it made the difference. She felt light—young—a little giddy

—and yet as if she were more than she had been before.

He was pouring another glass of champagne for her. "Please!" he interrupted her protest. "It is so beautiful with your dress—I mean your eyes."

They had a corner, those deep-cushioned seats against the wall. He turned directly to her, and together they raised their glasses. He was looking into her eyes and she, for the moment, into his— a dizzy and beautiful intimacy—the life from his eyes making her alive in a way she had never been alive. "Why, I am happy!" something in her said, thus explaining the great difference.

"Don't worry about the train," he told her. "I will drive you out home."

"Oh, but it is far."

"That's good."

"Beyond Chantilly."

"We will see the sun rise in the forest!"

"Oh, I couldn't—do that," Brook faltered.

"And have breakfast there."

"How can you drive me out home?" she demanded, clutching at anything that would make her practical.

"How? In my car. It is my brother's car," he explained, and they laughed.

He was telling her about his brother, his shipping business between Norway and France. "He thinks I am impractical," said Erik. "But I think he is.

He wants to be an explorer. Well, why doesn't he?"

"He has a family, perhaps," Brook ventured.

"Oh, yes—but look at my family."

"Your family!" Too late she knew she had been too dismayed.

"I married a Dane. Never marry a Dane."

"Where is—the Dane?" asked Brook, more lightly this time.

"Where should a Dane be? In Copenhagen, of course. Were you ever in Copenhagen?"

Brook had not been in Copenhagen. She must get that last train—*now*, certainly, she must get it!

"I once thought of organizing a movement to save Copenhagen from its sanity. But now I would prefer a movement to keep all Danes in Copenhagen, and let them be as sane as they please. It was a joke on me," he told her. "I saw a beautiful, impassive surface and thought there were smoldering fires. But there are no fires in Denmark."

"You said—family. Have you children?"

"A little girl. I fear she is stuffing herself with Danish pastry, but I can do nothing about it. Oh, well, the milk and cheese are good." But he looked troubled, as if the milk and cheese were not enough.

"Do you ever—see them?"

"I understand I am divorced."

"Oh!" And as this was too relieved she added,

rather coldly, "Doesn't one know whether or not one is divorced?"

"No, one doesn't, necessarily. But my brother seems to think I am divorced, and he usually gets such things straight. But why should I be talking of a dismal past, when I am sitting here with you?" Again he looked into her eyes, and again she could not at once look from his.

"*Please*, Brook," he entreated, when she spoke again of the train. "Have we ever been together before?"

"No," smiled Brook. "We have never been together before."

"For both of us, a number of years have gone by—"

"A number."

"And we were far apart. And now—we are here —close together." It seemed like him that as he said it he did not move closer, but left them in the consciousness of being close.

"Tell me—you are not an—an especial friend of that elderly Englishman who sat beside you to-night?"

The Colonel! To-morrow he was coming to visit her. Oh, she must go home and get some sleep! And because she did not want to go, stubbornly loyal to the Colonel, she said: "A very especial friend."

"How?" he demanded, indeed demanding now.

"My husband was ill a long time, and Colonel Fowler was especially good to me."

"Well, and why shouldn't he be? And what of it?"

She felt him alert now, coldly combative. It mattered to him! It commanded all of him, something to fight for; and because this was an intoxicant of which she must have more she said: "I think I am going to marry him."

"I think you are not!"

Like steel now his blue eyes, all of that driving energy right here. But all at once he seemed relieved. "How can you joke like that? It is not right."

"I am not joking. And I am thinking of marrying Colonel Fowler because it is right."

"I do not know what you are talking about. He is old."

"Not so very."

"And you are young."

She shook her head. "Not so very."

He leaned toward her. He put his hand out, but did not quite touch her hand. "Listen, Brook. My dear, listen to me. You are— But why should we sit longer in this stuffy place! Come. We will get the car. We will drive all through the forest. It will still be night. There will be stars through the trees. And then it will begin to change. We will see it change. For us, too, all things are changing. We will talk and talk as it changes—Iceland— Colorado, the years we have not had together. Maybe we will. It will be morning and we will have coffee together at an inn!"

CHAPTER XXXVI

SHE put in two lumps of sugar and held up the tongs with the third. She knew the Colonel always had two lumps and sometimes three. "This one?" she asked, holding it over the cup, and suddenly realizing how many times she had done just this in England—often in Bert's room, sometimes, Bert less well, down in the library— Colonel Fowler there with good counsel, giving a sense of support. The third lump always had a little the character of excess, an indulgence. If she were down-hearted, if it was cheer he would bring, relaxation of tension— "Yes, please," he would say heartily, as to say, "Well, why not?" To-day, "Thank you, no," said the Colonel to the third lump.

Sense of guilt had made her welcome warm; he was gradually thawing. She had feared he might not come, offended by her behavior the night before. She had worried, too, about Evans, fearing he might know it was seven when she got in that morning— what would a boy think of a mother who stayed out all night? "Oh, keep the car quiet as you can!" she had laughed to· Erik, as they drove up to the house. Marie was up. *"Madame!"* she cried, frightened as Brook let herself in, when she had

assumed Madame sleeping in her room. Brook
murmured something about a long party, a car that
had broken down. Marie's surprise had given way
to discreet excitement; when Brook saw herself in
the mirror she better understood her French serv-
ant's look. Yes, they liked such things; and no
wonder she had been astonished, so sober a house-
hold Marie had served. "Do not call me until
noon," Brook whispered. *"Mais non, Madame,"*
was the faintly reproachful reply, as to say, "Do
you think I would? Could she not first bring coffee
—chocolate? No, Brook had had coffee—where
the car broke down. She tiptoed past Evans' room,
and when they met at *déjeuner* he had been playing
tennis and did not know she had slept until one.

So everything was all right, and now she was
warmly gracious to the Colonel and Evans, knowing,
too, that she was beautiful to-day—flushed, eyes
alive, feeling youthful in the short pleated plaid skirt
and the smart orange sweater of fine soft wool.
Lightheartedly she took a cigarette.

"Haven't had one to-day," she laughed, but not
saying how many she had had last night, for they
smoked as they talked, leaving the highway for the
older roads of the forest. She smiled into the
languidly dissolving smoke of her cigarette. Erik
had been saying, "But I do not agree with Einstein
in that—" and telling where he did not agree with
him (poor Brook could not understand Einstein, to

say nothing of intricate disagreements) there had been a great jolt—he had run them into a tree! Going slowly, fortunately. Why had it seemed so funny, for in appearance at least, the car was damaged and Erik said his brother would not be greatly pleased.

But everything had been heightened in what it was —if funny, very funny; the trees never so tall— eloquent alone here in the last starlight, touched by the first dawn. There had been the wonder of words —never had words been so faithful, or of such beauty; she had a warm gratefulness to the words for thus letting them say the things to be said between them: a little boy's life in Iceland, his excitements at school, his greater excitement when he had worked something out by himself and found this filled a gap, or perhaps even corrected a mistake in what he had been taught. Excitement and quarrels in the university. He had been "disruptive" at Cambridge, Hélène's Sorbonne friend had said. Erik told her of losing his university position in Norway for "insisting on theories of his own." "They are not theories," he insisted to Brook, "for some of them I have established. And what," he demanded, "is more interesting, or more important, than a theory?"

Brook did not know what could be more interesting than a theory, unless it were this talk in the forest—finding themselves deep in the trees, coming together in everything they said: missionaries, mathematics; yes, we were coming to it now—a long time we had lived without knowing, soon we would be inside of life, not ignorant on a surface. Light waves. Did her mother's voice, then, still exist— on its way to some star—to that star up there to which she—Brook—now looked, in the forest of Chantilly, with a man of magic from Iceland—a man of grand excitements, of passion, timidities; violent, tender—yes, and lonely, too.

"How was the music last night?" she heard Evans asking.

"It was not music," said the Colonel.

"I liked it," said Brook, but not assertively, smiling.

"How can you like that which makes no sense?"

"I don't know, possibly it makes—another kind of sense."

"A thing makes or does not make sense."

"Think so?" asked Evans, as if thinking about it. Brook looked at him with new, keen interest. Perhaps Evans would like Erik.

Evans laughed. "Wonder which kind of sense we'll find in America, Mother."

"America?" asked the Colonel, and Brook could not reply, for in her, too, it was echoed with dismay —"America!"

She had forgotten! But—but that was incredible! She sat there helplessly. In the curious beauty of this day—a quality both thin and rich, nothing going farther back than last night—she had *forgotten* about going to America to see her father before he died!

"Oh!" Evans was sorry he had spoken of it. "I thought Mother had told you."

"I was going to now," said Brook.

"You are going to America?" The Colonel's voice refused to believe what it said.

Brook had no voice to affirm it. But she felt Evans looking at her. She said: "Yes."

"Now?" he asked. "At once?"

Evans waited for his mother to tell it. As she did not, he said for her, uncertainly: "As soon as we can get sailings; isn't that it, Mother?"

Again they both waited for her to speak. "Yes," she said.

"You see," Evans was explaining, "Mother's father, my Grandfather Evans, is very feeble, and wants to see Mother."

"Very feeble . . . wants to see Mother."

She knew that Colonel Fowler was watching her. "I am sorry you have this worry," he said, always kind when there was trouble. As she did not speak he added: "It is such a long way to go."

"Yes," she agreed.

"You feel you must really go at once?"

She hesitated. "I—I fear so."

"Mother's uncle wrote Mother might not see her

father if she did not come at once," Evans explained in lower tone, both of them assuming this strange manner was fear for her father, feeling about him.

Evans left them, and the Colonel was his old self now, as if difficulty had given him his place with her; indeed he was as one relieved, feeling perhaps that this explained things he had not understood, deciding her unnaturalness of the night before was nervousness, a seeking to forget, a not giving sign.

"You must not let this distress you," he said. "We can—we must plan it in a way that will not be—too hard for you." Yes, himself now, quiet, strong, because there was need of him. In command. And underneath this—excitement of which she was aware as he watched her, asking about her father. She knew what was in his mind, his idea of planning it in a way that would not be too hard for her. Seeing how she dreaded going alone, he would propose going with them, that he might manage everything, take care of her. She knew he would urge they be married at once.

CHAPTER XXXVII

SHE had told Erik she would be unable to see him for two or possibly three days. "Two or three days!" he cried, as if she had said two or three months. "Now—when we have just —found each other?"

"Yes," she said, "now—when we have just found each other." Wonderful she could speak it this way, as fact, for in the more usual terms— Hélène's terms—they had not yet "found each other." It was part of the wonder and great beauty of it, it was her pride that his excited insistence was not merely a man's desire to possess a woman who attracted him. It was—indeed herself, something in personal quality, made him want her, and made him want first to know her. To another it might seem strange how much of their talk had been of impersonal things, though none of it seemed impersonal, charged with an intimacy curiously profound. When they finally stopped at the inn in the forest, Madame was just making the fire and received them, first with astonishment, then gay indulgence.

Alone there in the little room: "Brook! Why are you named Brook?"

"A brook my mother loved," she told him. "It was there—there her love was. That is why I am here."

"Ah," he said, all that was himself now going to this, beautiful as he felt beauty in the story. Quite easily she had told him what she would not have believed she could tell any one—her mother's story. How grave he could be, how serious and tender in understanding! Her eyes had filled, for she had a feeling that never in her mother's whole life had she been understood as now by this man from Iceland, while they drank coffee at six in the morning and Madame, nodding and laughing over her fire, fried them eggs. "I was not good to her," Brook said. "Sometime I will tell you. When you know me better. You would not like me if I told you now."

"You will tell me later," he said; "when you want to tell me. But you could not make me not like you, Brook. You could not make me—not love you."

"Love me? You scarcely know me."

"I love you," was his reply, and just then *"Voilà!"* Madame had cried, with the eggs.

As they emerged from the forest, across the fields rose the one completed tower of the Senlis cathedral. They talked of why it had not been finished. Had faith gone? Was there some man who had visioned and worked for it, and had that

man died and no other cared enough to keep at
work the hundreds who must work? "It is eloquent, the one tower," she had said. "There is a
beauty in incompleted things." He was long silent;
then, "No!" he exploded. "Not if you see it that
way. Not if you see it that way while you are
doing it. If it is a beauty—it is a beauty must
overtake you—you running from it hard as you
can! We must fight for our work," he said, grim
now. "And we must not lose time." Then he was
telling her of something he suspected, of something
toward which he worked. "I am glad I was let out
from the university, for I might not have given up
the job soon enough, and I must go to China."

"China!" she had cried, and unashamed now of
her dismay.

"Oh, yes, but we will go together," he said, as if
there could be no question about this.

China? China was preposterous. Certainly she
could not go to China. There was something, some
secret; only from old manuscripts in China could
he verify a thing suspected. "And if I find this to
be true—!" He threw back his head and there in
the morning sun he was to Brook as a god—a god
from the North, going to China for an old secret.

"All of this was Norwegian," he said, waving his
hand as if possessing the country through which
they rode, and from it gaining added strength.
"The Norsemen came here. They were every-

where. They have always gone everywhere and taken as they liked. They were fools, though," he muttered, and for the moment thinking darkly.

They were in a Senlis street when he halted the car. "There is one thing you must promise me, or I will not stay away."

"What must I promise?"

"You must promise me you will not promise to marry this Colonel."

His eyes would not let her turn from him. She should say, "What right have you to ask that?" But she laughed: "I promise I will not promise him until—after I have seen you again."

He was not sure this was enough, then a change in his eyes, as if from the thought that after she had seen him again she would not want to promise —a pretty confident person, she thought, faintly resentful—confident, despite surprising diffidences.

At the door: "Good-by, Brook," he said, softly. "Good-by, Erik," was her low reply. A moment they looked into each other's eyes, then smiled— shy, happy, for the look had been like a kiss.

It seemed she was getting through the evening without the Colonel having his opportunity to talk with her. But her success here was not a pleasure, not kind to the old friend who visited her. The evening was not what he wanted, as she asked the Edwards over for bridge. "You don't much mind?" she asked, wanting to be as good to him as she could, and wishing she could indeed make him happy here with her, thinking always of his long kindness.

"As you say," he had answered stanchly. "Perhaps it will take your mind from the things that are troubling you."

Gratefully she caught at this. "Yes, bridge can do that, can't it?"

But the Edwards went early; Evans was not at home—over playing billiards with the Edwards boys. "How about a nightcap?" she asked, getting the whisky. How well she knew his habits, the things that would please him. Yes, this he liked, sitting with her before the fire, leisurely over his drink, she too sipping a little drink, and smoking. This is what her evenings would be, here would be the future, had it not been that last night her eyes met the eyes of a certain man—a very strange and no doubt irresponsible man. But something—what was it?—had happened between them, and the world changed.

Yet she had not said to herself that she was not going to marry Colonel Fowler; she was not facing it. Something had happened. Just what she did not know, or what it might become. How could she think—just now?

"Tired?" Andrew asked.

"I was up late last night," she confessed.

"You have made some new friends?"

"Yes."

"I do not like to think of your being alone," he began. "You are too—"

"Surely not too young," she laughed.

"Too attractive."

O dear! What a reason for marrying, because one was "too attractive!" But she disliked herself for these surreptitious critical thoughts.

"About this—going to America," he began.

But the front door banged.

"That you, dear?"

Evans joined them.

She talked spiritedly, doing her best at keeping him, but he felt he was interrupting the Colonel's talk with her. After a little he said he was going to turn in.

"Good-night, sir."

"Good-night, Evans."

There was a nice feeling between them. She knew Andrew had been disappointed by the interruption, yet he had not let the boy feel this, but talked genially about his game of billiards. Evans respected and liked his father's old friend. Good for a boy to have a man at home. In the years just ahead how much he might need a man to turn to. Could one dismiss all that—the Brook who had been responsible through years asked herself— just because of one mad night? One mad night.

Was it a madness exploding into the future, opening a future? Madness? Life. Through years
there had been so little; there would be little now,
little that to her was life—nothing, indeed, if she
did this reasonable thing, making a home for herself and her boy. And yet, looking into the years
still farther ahead, years that waited, beyond all
chance of the dizzy stern beauty that was "life."
. . . Yes, of those years, too, she must think. But
trying to think of them, sitting on here with the
man who would surely talk to her if she did not
at once say good-night, other things were being
said to her, things said by her very blood.

She wanted to go to bed, to be alone with the
wonder of her feeling. She could say, "To-morrow
we will have a good visit. I'll be more fit after
I make up for late hours." She could say this.
He would accept it. It didn't seem fair. How
could she be anything but generous with this man
who had been so fair and generous with her? Further evasions were unworthy. She must meet him
as honestly as she could. Though what would that
be? What was there for her to say?

"I am sorry you must go to America now."

"Yes, I am sorry to go—just now."

"But of course you must."

"It seems so," she murmured.

"If your father wants you. And he hasn't seen
you for—?"

"Twenty years," said Brook.

"Is it possible!"

To her it did not seem possible.

"You must go," he said decisively. "It would be hard for you afterwards, if you did not go."

"Yes."

"One's father. Mine died when I was twenty. One's own father—"

And you do not know, was the pain in Brook's heart, how much more it is than—one's own father!

He leaned forward, fire and candlelight kindly to his face, where stronger light now showed flesh not youthful, uncertainties in modeling, color of an aging man. This sympathetic light, feeling, gave a leaner, more vital look as he said: "Let me go with you."

He put down the glass he held. "I have loved you for a long time, Brook. You know that."

"Yes," she was compelled to acknowledge. "And been good to me."

"I want to be good to you always. To take care of you. I want to be good to Bert's boy—and yours. I do not any longer want to be outside the right to do this. I love you," he whispered. "Oh —so long. I want you, Brook!"

"Want"—want?—but that meant—and she wanted . . . He was less steady now as he leaned nearer. Oh, what could she do—*now*—when all of her wanted another!

"Andrew," she said, "my dear friend—so good to me. But—something has happened."

"Happened? What has happened?"

"Something to make me uncertain."

"But you can't be uncertain," he said, a little sharply. "Not now. You have decisions to make."

"Yes. I must make them," said Brook, faintly.

He searched her face; she felt sorry for him, disappointed, left thus in the dark. "Oh, I am sorry," she said.

"I think it is that you are disturbed about your father. But here you must let me help you," he went on, surer now, as always when helping. "We will go together."

"It is not my father." She could not leave him so mistaken.

There was a pause. "Something—new?" he asked.

She nodded.

He got up, several times cleared his throat, moved around, less gentle now.

"This man you went away with last night?"

She was startled. She had not meant to tell him about Erik. She had hoped he did not know, though she might have known Hélène would tell him!

"Yes," she said, a little defiantly, though the defiance was mostly toward Hélène.

"Something of a ne'er-do-well, isn't he?"

"A pretty brilliant ne'er-do-well," she defended.

But immediately her solicitude went back to him, sagging as he stood there by the fire, thinking of this much more youthful man.

"I am sorry," said Brook. "I hadn't meant to— talk of it. You see I—I didn't know him until last night." She laughed a little wildly.

"You did not know him until last night," he repeated, slowly, as if giving her a chance to correct the incredible words.

But feeling herself challenged, "No," said Brook, more strongly.

He was looking at her. "I would not have believed it," was all he could say. "You always seemed so—so wise."

"Too wise, perhaps. If you call it—wise."

He sat down near her. "Listen. You've lost your head. It's incredible—*you*. But now think of it as you yourself would have thought of it— before last night."

"Nothing very bad happened last night," said Brook, sparring like a girl being scolded.

"I am sure of that," he said, firmly. "I know you."

"Oh, *do* you?" thought Brook, but holding her hands tight together, not wanting to say more.

"There is much to consider, when one is thinking of—all the rest of one's life."

"That is true!" something from her cried, and not from things he would have her consider.

"It was—an escapade. All right. Why not?" he went on bravely. "All those quiet years. The years ahead won't need to be so quiet. But come now. Use your good sense. A little fling—is that to count in arranging all the rest of your life?"

Arranging all the rest of your life! Why did it sound like laying out a corpse for a funeral?

"We've known each other—it's about eighteen years, isn't it, since Bert brought you to Constantinople?"

Eighteen years. One night! But time . . . Other ways of looking at time. It was as if she and Erik, last night, had been taken into all the time there was and ever could be, had become of it, and could have from it. As if an opening had been made in time—for them.

"I've respected you so, Brook. Your dignity in all that—long hardship."

Then he took for himself an advantage. "Which would Bert want you to do?"

"You know," she answered. "And so should not have asked."

"No," he accepted the rebuke.

And yet—*would* he? Would Bert? If he knew all? Bert who had wanted to "rescue" her—for life, and grieved because he had not been able to do so.

"What about going to America—to see your father?"

Yes! What about it? Oh, there was so *much*, and suddenly exhausted she felt herself trembling inside. She could not check it, she was sobbing. Covering her face—"I don't *know*. I tell you I don't—I can't—"

He did not let her off. "Did he ask you to marry him?"

She raised her head, though knowing her face was disfigured with angry, exhausted tears. "What right have you to ask that?"

"The right of one who would protect you," he answered, very much in command now. "He is married, isn't he?"

"He thinks he's divorced," said Brook, wanly.

" 'Thinks he's divorced!' " He laughed with hard scorn. But after another scoffing laugh he said, "Go to bed now, Brook. You're tired out. Everything will be different to-morrow. To-morrow we will arrange about the trip to America," he said firmly, as if none of this had happened.

CHAPTER XXXVIII

THE Colonel said he would have to go in to Paris that day, but that he would like to come back for dinner and stop with them again that night. "Then I must return to England," he said, "for at least a few days." He had his manner of having taken command, and not in a way that opened his affairs to discussion. He did not say, "I must go to England before we are married and sail for America," so Brook could not say, "We are not going to be married and sail for America." She was glad enough not to talk of things—for what was she to do about America? Like going away from life when one has just found life! She tried not to think of it, telling herself she could arrange nothing until she had again seen Erik. If Andrew took it upon himself to go in and see about sailings—he should not have done it! She was not a child, to have her affairs taken out of her hands.

But also there was Evans. "Mother, shouldn't we be getting ready?"

"Getting ready?"

"To go to America."

"Oh, that won't take long."

"Aren't there things we ought to buy?"

"We have clothes enough, haven't we?"

"But things we'll need on the steamer. People always seem to be buying rugs and baskets of things for journeys," he laughed. As she did not reply: "And presents."

"Presents?"

"Shouldn't we take presents to Grandfather Evans and those cousins we'll stop with?"

She found this exasperating, yet just so would she herself have been thinking it—if she hadn't run away to dance with Erik Helge.

"We'll do all that after the Colonel goes," she told Evans.

"He'd like to do it with us. And what about passports?" he demanded.

"Please, Evans! I'm very busy to-day. I—I'm trying to think something out."

"Sorry," he said shortly.

She went running after him when he started for his lesson. He studied Latin and Greek with a young German professor then living in Senlis. "Got your papers, dear? Know your verbs this time?"

He remained a little out of sorts with her.

How like a family they seemed, in the library after dinner that night. Evans was wrestling with a knotty passage in Cæsar. "Let me have a look at him," the Colonel suggested. "I have remained somewhat acquainted with the old boy." He read it aloud with no little authority, helping Evans through the tangle. Evans asked questions about Cæsar. Was he really so good? Yes, Colonel Fowler pronounced he was good. They talked of other great generals, of Napoleon. Evans was interested. He had a respectful manner which was more than courtesy, more than liking. Here was a man he looked up to; and in character the kind of a man a boy should admire, she supposed—the safest place for respect.

Evans' school books brought the picture of herself in the kitchen of their Santa Clara house. "Oh, *dear!*" she would cry from her difficulties, and her father or her mother might try to help her, they would all talk of what a thing meant. That life was far away. That life was forever gone. And the father who had been good to her through those days waited for her now—waited for her to come, before it would be too late. Here in this room were two men who loved her—a very young man, a man much older, who assumed she would go to the father who had long awaited her—took for granted she would be loyal to that home which was no longer. Here beside her were two who wanted to help her in this, affectionately supporting.

Her place seemed with them, in the things they felt she should do. Outside that . . .

The bell sounded. Marie said a gentleman was here to see Madame.

"Ask him—" But wondering why he had not

given his name—*could* it be? She rose and went into her little salon, where Marie had taken the visitor. Erik stood there.

"Shouldn't I have?" he began contritely.

"It is against our agreement," she said, but too glad to see him to reproach or consider the embarrassment.

"I know. I only meant to walk by the house, thinking about you. I think and think about you, Brook." He held out his hands, and she took them. They stood so for a moment, silent.

"And I thought he might have gone," Erik smiled. "I thought, as things weren't—to his liking, he might have gone."

"No. My friend has not gone."

He searched her face. "I have worried about you, fearing you were troubled. You have been troubled! What right has he to make it hard for you?"

She glanced to the half-open door. He moved to close it.

"No. No, I can't—stay in here with you; not to-night."

"Mayn't your friends call upon you?"

"Certainly. But I told you—"

"I know. But I was so lonely without you. It seemed I couldn't go through another night without seeing you."

That this should be true, and what she saw, felt

in him, as much as his words, made it true—the wonder of it was greater than anything else.

"Take me where you are. Why not? What's wrong with me?" he laughed. "I know some very nice people."

Suddenly defiant, loyal to him, and, above all, not wanting him to go: "We are in the library," she told him, leading the way.

"Colonel Fowler, this is Mr. Helge. . . . My son Evans."

Now Erik Helge sat with them in the library. Colonel Fowler had received him in the official manner of one who anticipates relations will at any moment be broken and who is not there to sustain them. Erik sat at an end of the long table before which Evans was seated with his books. He spoke with him of what he was doing. Evans, she saw, was interested in this unusual-looking man who did not say the expected things about a boy's studies. Erik was disposed to treat the Colonel as an insurgent nation might a deposed monarch, as to say, "Oh, let him keep his manner, if he likes. What's the difference, when it can't do anything?"

"But too bad they give you such stupid stuff to read," Erik was saying. "There's a lot of interesting Latin."

"Cæsar is not stupid," said Colonel Fowler, his eye going just above the top of his own boot and stopping just a little short of Erik.

"I found him so."

"That does not make it so."

"It makes him so for you though, doesn't it?" said Evans pleasantly.

"Cæsar is not stupid," Colonel Fowler repeated.

A silence. "I've forgotten whether he is or not," Brook filled the gap.

Erik opened the Greek reader. "But here is the language. Perhaps I am partial to it because it was the language of Anaxagoras."

"I'm not up on him," laughed Evans.

"He had a great head on his shoulders. We haven't had a better head since we began having them."

Brook, seated near them, took the book and ran her finger along the letters. "I never studied Greek, but I wish I did know it. I like the look of the letters. As if a key that could unlock beautiful secrets."

This pleased Erik, who looked at her in his way of seeing, of continuing to see. Brook flushed, aware that Evans was right beside her, that the Colonel now regarded them.

"Do you think Greek is a better language than Latin?" Evans asked, pleasantly conversational.

"Greek is the best language there has been in the world," said Erik.

Colonel Fowler cleared his throat. "English is

the best language there has been in the world," he observed quietly.

"English is good," Erik began, cordially, "for a mongrel tongue. But you couldn't spoil any language that drew so much from the Norwegian."

"Are you Norwegian?" Evans inquired.

"That," remarked Colonel Fowler, "was obvious."

"Mr. Helge is from Iceland," Brook told Evans. There followed spirited inquiries into the climate and winter sports of Iceland.

Colonel Fowler was sitting too still, eyes fixed on nothing.

He moved ever so slightly, looking toward Erik but not at him. "You are a university man, I believe?"

"Oh, yes. I have more or less—visited around in universities. England—Germany—here and there."

Color just stained the Colonel's slightly sagging face. "You are a university teacher, I believe."

"I have been. But I was fired." Evans giggled. "Fired," Erik told him, "for heretical utterances about the second law of thermo-dynamics. I am grateful to thermo-dynamics, for now I can do my own work. It is hard," he told Brook, "to do one's own work in a university."

The Colonel, seated in an easy-chair, moved one shoulder away from the group at the table. It was sitting so he said as if he had suddenly thought of it, said with particular distinctness: "Oh, by the way, I inquired about your sailings to-day."

Brook felt Erik's eyes upon her, felt the color heightening in her face.

"When will we go?" Evans asked eagerly.

"There is a White Star boat on the twelfth—that is a week from to-morrow. Anything before that would be the French line."

"And you think we should go on an English boat?" Evans asked.

"I think so."

Brook was unable longer to refuse to meet Erik's eyes. When she saw them she moved to put out her hand, then knew she could not do this. "Sailings?" he murmured.

"Mother and I are going to America," Evans told him.

"You—are going to America?" He said it low, not taking his eyes—incredulous, hurt—from her face.

"I—perhaps," was all she could say.

"Mother's father is in failing health," Evans explained.

Erik laughed. She knew Evans must be looking at him in surprise. Colonel Fowler turned ever so slightly, as if on guard against a discourtesy.

"Your father—is an old man, isn't he?" Erik asked excitedly.

"Certainly," Brook murmured.

"When I saw you—the other night, you did not speak of going to America."

She wished he would not do this—show hurt before the man who wanted to hurt him. But apparently it mattered too much to consider this lesser thing.

"I did not think to mention it," Brook said, trying to let her look make up for what she could not say, trying to say with her eyes: "Wait. Trust me."

But he could not. "You knew you were about to sail for America and—did not think to mention it?"

Colonel Fowler uttered a preliminary sound. "Why should Mrs. Leonard mention it—if she did not choose to?"

Thus roused—against him, for Erik: "I did not mention it because—when I was with you—I forgot it." She looked at him to reinforce her words. There was silence in the room. Then, embarrassed, Evans whistled under his breath.

"But you are going?" Erik's voice was low, to her alone.

"I don't know." She, too, spoke very low; embarrassed by this intimacy. "I don't know," she repeated, in more usual voice.

Erik did not take his eyes from her face. He made little attempt at concealing what he felt.

"Why—Mother!" Evans said. "I thought it was all settled."

"Of course your mother is going," observed

Colonel Fowler. "How could she refuse to go to her father, who is dying, and needs her? But she is not compelled to discuss that here."

"It was not I, nor was it Mr. Helge," said Brook, trembling now with dismay, "who began discussing it here."

"Your sailings," he murmured. "I thought you would be glad to know."

"And what about passports?" Evans demanded.

"Exactly. We must all go in in the morning. You have not American citizenship, you know. You are British."

Erik rose.

"Oh, I am sorry—you are going," Brook told him. "I am—indeed sorry."

He said good-night to Evans, barely articulated a good-night to Colonel Fowler, who punctiliously articulated a reply. Brook went with him into the hall; her hand on his arm guided him to the salon.

"When we are together—I can make it all clear."

Roughly he took her arm. "We must be together to-night! Yes. Do not say no! Oh, you cannot do that, Brook. Leave it—all night—to-morrow—until to-morrow night—like this. You cannot leave it—between you and me—like this!"

"But I cannot leave here to-night."

"Yes. They will go to bed. Then you will come out and meet me. I will be waiting for you."

"*Erik!* I cannot do—that sort of thing."

"What 'sort of thing'? You cannot do *this* sort of thing—leaving it, between us, like this. Listen. Listen, Brook. I will be there—across the ramparts —the path leading down to the war cemetery. It will not be far for you to come alone. I can see you—almost all the way. I will wait—I'll wait until morning, if I have to. But come soon, Brook. Do not leave it—between us—like this!"

He held her arms, looking hard into her face. And seeing what he felt—yes, he was right, she could not leave it, between them, like this.

"As soon as I can," she said.

CHAPTER XXXIX

NOW they had gone to their rooms. "I will say good-night," she had said, soon after Erik left. Colonel Fowler could not expect her to sit talking with him to-night, after his discourtesy to her visitor. He was apprehensive; it came faintly, unwillingly, into his manner as he said good-night. He would like a chance to talk with her. She would not grant it. "That's a funny fellow," Evans remarked, and received no reply from his elders. "Nice though," he added.

The two had remained for a time in the library. Evans put on a record. Upstairs Brook got out heavier shoes, her coat. It seemed long to wait, though less than an hour. They came up together, talked for a moment in the hall, Evans asking the Colonel if his reading-light was all right. Doors closed. Some moving around for a time, then the house was still. But she must wait a little longer.

What a thing for her to be doing! "At *my* age." She had never done such a thing in her life. Yes, yes she had. In Santa Clara, to meet Tony. Then it was her mother she left unknowing in the house. Though not unknowing, pretending to be, because she wanted her to meet Tony, because she wanted her to go toward happiness, toward life.

She would go down the back stairway and so would not need to pass their rooms. She could go through the garden and out that gate in the wall, then they could not see her, if one of them should look from a window. Undignified. Absurd. Erik was waiting for her. He cared like this!

Now. Very softly. She was out the side door, through the garden, through the gate and crossing the street into the trees that make a boulevard on the ramparts. This must be the path he—

"Brook!" His arms were around her. "You came!" He kissed her.

"Tell me, Brook! I must know now. Do you love me?"

"I love you."

They moved down the path, passing many graves just alike—graves of men who would not love again —found a road that crossed a stream, stood on this bridge, looking down into the water, hearing it.

"It is not true," he said, after only the water had spoken. "You will not go away— now."

She held his arm close. She did not want to go away now.

"But you see—my father, he is not my father, not really."

She told him more than she had told before. The little boy trampled before his eyes. "A slow, dry man, always old. Mother never loved him. She could not. No love in his life, except what there was from me. Never let me know! Now he is going. Going from our world. Wants to see me—before he goes."

She was weeping as they moved along the road, across the open country before the forest.

"Yes, yes, dear. I understand." He saw it. "That makes it hard." He was tender with her as they walked through the country where every one else slept, this still night of stars.

"Why do you love me?" she asked.

"Why? Does one know why?"

"You scarcely know me."

"I feel you, I feel what you are. Yes, I know you."

"But you love me as if I were—a girl. I am thirty-eight years old," Brook said bravely.

"You are, dear? You do not seem that, for youth has not gone—not *willing* to go—from you. Yet I think it is the years I love in you. In you is living itself—as a rare essence. I know how you will love me, Brook—after the years not love. It is myself! I am thinking of myself! But also—I am thinking of you. I want to make you happy —good, *good*, Brook. I want to—" he laughed, "rescue you—from all that is not life. How could you say I do not know you? I felt you in your eyes—when your eyes met mine, we listening to

the not very successful music—felt all the stubborn
old things lighted into life by the eyes of Brook!
Others live in you—there to give, to be fought. It
makes you wonderful, darling. When I hold you
I can live with the whole great past! No, do not
laugh. I am crazy—yes," he, too, laughed, a short
laugh of happy excitement— "I am crazy, but I
know what I am talking about!"

"I will be getting older," said Brook, with all
her courage.

"Yes, and that makes these years—God's gift
to us. What God gives us we take when He gives,
or forever lose."

At this they stood there in the great trees, holding each other's hands.

"You say God, Erik," said Brook gravely. "But
do you believe in God?"

"I used to mathematically prove there could be
no God. When you go farther, into dizzy things
I have worked with, when you make a leap, then
look back to the truth into which you could not
have worked your way—the leap, perhaps that is
God. Such times I have had a feeling of something in me more than myself, and so, until I know
better, as a working hypothesis," he laughed, "I am
willing to say God. Listen to the trees."

"They are not afraid to say God," Brook murmured.

"How beautiful—when your face lifts like that!

To say you look young—that is unfair to you. The young can look young—so easily, so often without meaning. How can one have beauty who has not gone through things? You have wondered—haven't you, my Brook? Far away in Colorado—in the East with the missionaries—through bewildered years in England—in loneliness, in emptiness, you have wondered. And believed. And waited. And would have foregone. But that you shall not do! That shall not be. And when I make you mine and make you happy—now—make you mine and make you happy—life has won a victory! There will be rejoicings in Heaven to-night for one who is saved! And I—" suddenly different, for changes were swift in him, now humble, grateful, burying his face against her— "I—at last—have love."

"You must have had love, Erik," she said, gently caressing his head. "You."

"Not much. Not as I wanted love. Perhaps I asked too much. There is love that—does nothing for you at all." His fingers followed her face, as if to know it better, as if to make it of himself. "Brook," he said softly. "She named you Brook."

"But what can I do, dear?" she asked, still fighting the miracle of her happiness, and more troubled than before, knowing now what was here. "It is too late not to go. Even my son feels I must go to my father."

They had walked on, deeper into the forest. As

before, they stood still, listening to the trees; though it was not as if they paused—listening, but as if halted—stilled—for some old message, some meaning.

"That is hard, about your father. Yes, life can be hard. You know that. It is deep in your eyes. And we must be brave. You have been brave. In the right way, always? Isn't there—another courage?"

"Another courage?" she whispered, close to him, his arms around her, as if indeed for strength.

"Your father is an old man, Brook. At the end of things. For us there are years ahead—not too many. These are the years for love and love is here." (Where had she heard that before? Some one had said that before!) "It is *now*—or die not having lived! Oh, how can one *argue* it?" he cried, as if suddenly angry. "I love you. Do not again ask me why. How do I know why? It is—a leap. Together we will know glory! Come, darling—come—for such years as God gives us! Madness and miracles there will be—a dizzy beauty that will bite like frost. Hardships. Perhaps at the last we will walk barefoot in China! But now—oh, now—"

"Oh, no, Erik! Not now!" For the imminence of life long denied frightened her, and all old resistances struggled against the love she desired.

"Now!" he would say, with the solemnity of passion richer than deep music, strong as the sea. "You

—me. Then it can never be any other way. No, dear—do not cry. I will be good to you! Brook, my little one!"

Deep in the forest, as if they were alone on earth, as if all life behind them had been that this might be—the noble trees—the far stars—now it was Brook Evans knew love.

CHAPTER XL

THREE days she put off her talk with Evans. She would tell him to-night.

Something of it she had told Colonel Fowler that next morning. "No, I am not going to Paris with you. Never mind the passports; I will attend to things."

He was sorry, he said, saying it with difficulty, if he had seemed rude to—that man. He confessed he disliked him. He seemed impertinent.

As she did not unbend: "You are angry?"

"Yes. Oh, that is not fair," she was obliged to admit. "It is not just that I am angry. It is— the whole thing." She said it. "I do not love you, I love him."

"I cannot believe it," he said, low, slowly. "Love him? You do not know him."

"I love him."

"You are—not going to your father?"

"That is for me to decide."

"I beg your pardon," he said coldly, but so broken she cried: "I am sorry!"

"But it is true," she repeated, as he waited, hoping.

And so he left her, he who had been her stanch friend through years. She watched him from the door—moving a little more slowly; erect, though with effort. With him went sure years, respect, a home. And she knew that this was true.

"To-morrow," she said to Evans, as they sat by the library table, "we will go in and see about your passport."

"Have you got yours?"

"No."

"See about our passport, you mean."

She leaned a little across the table. "Dear, there is something I want you to do for me."

He waited—her boy. "Yes, Mother?"

"I want you to go alone."

"Why—Mother!" was all he could say.

"I cannot leave here now. I—do not want to."

"Really?" he asked, uncertainly.

"And I do not even want you to ask me why. Oh, you see," she said, her hands out toward him, "there is a very great deal I am asking of you."

"Why, that's all right," said Evans. "But it is you Grandfather wants to see."

Brook's eyes filled, as always now when she thought of a very old man, waiting. "Yes, he wants to see me. And"—she said it, making herself know that it was true—"and I am not going."

Even in that moment of much feeling—"He has good form," she was thinking of her boy who, not

understanding, merely waited for what she wished
to tell him.

"I cannot go. I have decided I cannot. I want
to send you in my place. I want to send my son to
my father because I shall never see him again."
She covered her face with her hands and, though
quietly, was sobbing.

"Mother," murmured Evans. "It seems," he ventured, "if you—want to see him so much—you had
better go."

She shook her head, in a moment had cleared
her eyes, could face him again.

"To see you—that will make up for it. It will
mean more to him, perhaps, than to have seen me."

"I suppose he'd like to see us both," Evans
laughed.

Brook frowned in order not to cry again. "Yes."

He did then ask a question. "Are you staying
because of the Colonel?"

"No."

"You're not going to—"

"No."

He looked at her. "Really, Mother? He
seemed awfully nice this time."

"Yes. In his way."

"He was always—good to us."

"Yes."

"But, Mother," he looked troubled, "will you be
here—all alone, then?"

She did not want to tell him. To tell it now—talk about it, explain, this she could not do. She must leave it the miracle it was. "Perhaps soon I can make it clear," she said. "Though even then, it may not be clear to you. If it is not, I ask you —I ask you, darling boy—because of the years we have had together—because of all we have gone through together—to form no hasty judgment. I ask you to say to yourself—I do not understand this now, but perhaps I will understand when I am older." Again tears were running down Brook's face. "Then think about it again, darling, when you are yourself near forty. If I am not around then, think about it—do that for me! And perhaps then you will say—as I say now to my mother—" But she could not say it. Her head went down to the table, sobbing as he had never seen her cry.

"Mother!" the boy whispered, and went around to her side of the table—put a diffident arm around her, for he was reticent. Not raising her head she took his hand, held it close.

"Well—there!" she exclaimed, getting up almost briskly. "Perhaps that is over." She moved around, cleared her eyes, blew her nose, went to the mirror, said, "Heavens!" took out her little silver box, powdered, touched her lips, her cheeks, took a cigarette.

"It will be an adventure, Evans, going alone. You have been so much with me." They began to make plans, the journey taking form in practical terms.

But it was different—an adventure to fear—when she stood with him in his cabin on the ship. She must go ashore in a few moments. Her boy—her baby—going thousands of miles alone. He had not been away from her, except at school. She was sending him to a strange country, a country which had become something she herself knew nothing about. She was sending him away from her! Would she ever have him again? What was she doing, she would ask herself, frightened, but keeping quiet, cheerful. She must not break down, sending him away dismayed.

Old missionary friends of hers would "help Evans through New York."

"I am sure you will be all right."

"Of course."

But just what was he feeling? She looked at him, trying to know. He had taken this upon himself for her. He appeared to want to go. If he were appalled, he did not show it. But she did not know what he was feeling. Would she ever again know what he was feeling?

"You will give Father—much love." She stood with her hand on the knob, her chin quivering.

"Yes. And I'll—make him feel all right about everything."

"He—he may seem—not attractive to you. So

old. Different from people you have known. Will you be—darling, will you be very good to him, for my sake, because—more than I can say—more than I have told you—he was—so good to me?"

"Of course, Mother," he assured her.

She had wondered—should she tell Evans? Before he went should she tell him the whole story? Perhaps it would interest him, making him especially good to his grandfather. But she remembered how it had repelled her, and now, soon she herself might have something to tell him that would surprise, shock. No. She had never told Evans' father. Never told Bert. Did she owe it to some one long dead—called Joe—to let his grandson know he *was* his grandson? *No.* Evans was *Father's* grandson. She would not have any other thing in the boy's mind when he went back where something had happened long ago.

"Remember that the gray robe is for Father. It is the brown one is for Uncle Willie."

"Yes, Mother. I think I have it all straight," he said cheerfully. He was helping her through the good-by.

She asked so much of him. "How can I—? I should not have let you—"

"Mother," he broke in, a trifle impatiently. "What's the matter? What's the matter with *me?*" he went on, more humorously. "I'm 'most eighteen years old. Can't I cross the ocean if I want to?"

"Yes,—yes, dear," she murmured, gratefully. "You will—take care of yourself, though?"

"No—oh, no," he said. "I expect to jump overboard as soon as you've left the steamer."

They laughed.

"Good-by, Evans."

"So long, Mother."

"You look like my mother," she said, holding his hands. "You might write me little stories you may hear about her."

"I'll do that." He led her on deck, talking cheerfully.

After he had kissed her good-by, put her in the tender, had himself started back, out of the way of others, she displeased the boatman by running back up the steps. She took Evans' arm, leading him away from the others.

"If there should be—I know there will be—flowers growing along the brook, gather some of them and take them to my mother's grave."

"I will, Mother."

"They must be from the brook—right alongside the brook!"

"I understand. Flowers growing by the brook."

"And—think about her, Evans. Let her—let her come to life in your mind."

"Yes—yes, Mother. And now—they are calling —you must go."

From shore she saw him standing a little by

himself. She pressed her hands to her mouth, then arms extending far as they would reach to the child she would not see for— For how long? How long?

Unsteadily she walked away.

It was at the café on the second street Erik would be waiting for her. That had been good of him— to propose coming up to drive her back. Until now she had not known how good it was. He, better than she, knew how much she would need him now. To leave Evans alone on that ship—she alone in this town—thinking through the ride back to Paris —yes, it was good of Erik. Suppose he should not be there, some misunderstanding, trouble with the car. It seemed everything else in the world had fallen away—and if now he were not here—

From across the street she saw him at a sidewalk table—writing, or was it figuring, making a design. He was absorbed in what he did and she stood watching him—a little of disappointment, something of fear, when he remained deep in what he was doing, his eyes not searching the street for her. If it were she sitting there waiting for him, she would not be able to conceal how anxious her look. But of course it was different with him. He had this passion in his work. It would often be like this. She would not have it otherwise; she loved him for this, she told herself, as across the street she halted, watching him. She had said to Erik—diffidently:

"You couldn't go with me?" "Just now everything depends on this," he explained. "If I can put this through, within the next month, then I am expecting to be given the money for China." This was from one of the funds for experimental work. It would give three years of his own work.

Erik looked up the street then, but not over where she stood, half concealed by others. His eyes reached far as he could see, as if thinking she should be coming soon. She was in his mind now. There was warmth, something of triumph in knowing he was thinking, not of these others who passed, but of her. He drank some beer, turned again to his papers. Those people around him—they did not know who he was, what he did, felt. She knew. To her he would tell of himself, wanting her to know. There was a curious intimacy in seeing him just across the street, he among strangers, she among strangers, and knowing that in a moment they would be together. He had taken off his hat and was twisting his hair as he worked. In a new way, she knew that she loved him. All of these people around him, all the world, might turn against him—she loved him! What was it he had said, extravagantly: "At the last we may walk barefoot in China." If even that were true—yes, she would fight for him, suffer, let go what must! Even the greatest danger she faced. Hers not the arrogance of youth. Forever? No, very probably it could not be forever.

If it could be but a few years—if it could be but one year—that she would have had—and then all the rest of her life . . .

As she was crossing the street the thought became a picture of her mother. "Yes," Brook said. "Yes, Mother. I think I understand now."

He looked up and saw her, rose with loving eagerness. *This* moment!—this welcoming look in his eyes—if it should be this alone, then all else blotted out—this she had had. And this next moment, as now he held her hands, searching her face to see how it had been with her, wanting to reach what it was she felt.

It was as if he paused before what he saw in her eyes, pain thus conquered by a certain valiant understanding, paused before the love she brought him.

"Brook!"

"Yes, Erik."

What did it mean?

They were together.

BOOK FIVE

CHAPTER XLI

UNCLE WILLIE'S wife, Aunt Agnes, had invited the relatives for Sunday dinner— "so's we can all get acquainted." To Evans there seemed no end to this getting acquainted with relatives. Not only Grandfather, Uncle Willie, Aunt Agnes—but Uncle Willie's daughter Grace, her children, and Uncle's son Frank all of them lived in this house. It was a house ugly in appearance, Evans thought, but they were very proud of "the improvements."

"Had to have more room—after Caleb came back, then Grace with her young-ones. That's how come we raised the roof," his Uncle explained, showing him what was the old part. There was no need to point this out, for the second story siding made the lower part very old. "Too bad," his Uncle said, "ought to have covered up the whole thing, but building's expensive now." Evans was about to say he liked the old part best, but refrained, for he was learning what not to say.

The new wing of the house was concrete, making the old part still older. But the ell, his grandfather's room, was untouched. "That used to be

Naomi's, that was your grandmother's room," his Uncle told him. "She set great store by it." Evans liked this room, but too bad they had built the concrete garage so near.

It was Aunt Rosie's folks were coming, but first they all went to church, all except Aunt Agnes, who stayed home to get dinner. There had been a long dispute as to whether Grace should not stay home and help. They had a way of talking to one another from different rooms, which made the disputes, though not angry, loud-voiced. Mother would not like this. Perhaps just as well Mother had not come, Evans more than once thought, especially when he had to look at his grandfather, who, as Frank said, slobbered. "No, now you go right along to church, Gracie, same as always—what with all we did yesterday, this dinner's going to be nothing at all for me to manage, and you to take hold when you get back." Aunt Agnes prevailed, as usual. She was a strong, determined woman. "Ma's a manager," they would say. Kind about things, but as if never pausing to let the kindness mean anything, never giving the moment a chance to be something of itself.

Evans had been little by himself; their idea of his having a good time was that he should never be alone. "Now, don't you go get homesick," Aunt Agnes would admonish. "Plenty here for you to be with, and all wants to be with you, too. Just you get acquainted." It was a June morning. He had heard an oriole. He would like to have struck out by himself, away from the town—across fields and over hills, a good tramp. But they wanted to "introduce him to the church folks."

Every one talked at once as to who should go in Frank's Chevrolet and who in Pa's Ford. Evans would have preferred the open Ford, but as the visitor he was given a place in the closed car, with his grandfather and Grace. Uncle Willie had children in his Ford, and he was to pick up a churchgoer who "had nothin' to do with but a horse and buggy."

"I'll go slow," Uncle Willie called to Frank, "so's you won't be too far behind." They laughed, quite as if this were a new joke among them.

Grandfather sat in front with Frank. "Well, your mother used to be a good hand to go to church," he turned to Evans. "Many's the Sunday morning her and me's set out across the valley for our meeting-house in Santa Clara. Naomi, she—well she'd stay at home to get the dinner." He turned to Grace, as if explaining something, and he seemed to grow excited, for his head went back and forth and it was as if the things he thought he was saying didn't come.

"Yes, Uncle Caleb," said Grace, soothingly, "just like Ma's doing now."

"That's right!" His voice came now, high, almost a cackle. "That's right." He kept on chuckling beyond any reason for it, his head moving back and forth.

"You see?" Grace murmured. Just tapped her temple, nodded, smiling indulgently. "Now this part of the town's all new," she explained brightly to Evans. "All this used to be country."

"I should think it did!" His grandfather suddenly turned around, in a crafty way, as if surprising them. But he turned back, adding, "I should think it did!" and pulling up his shoulders, as if he would have them protect his bent head.

There were some real pretty houses, Grace thought; mostly bungalows though, and more and more apartment buildings. Every few blocks they passed one of the violent red filling-stations.

The church itself was not unlike a too large bungalow. It was new—everything modern, Grace said. Evans' eyes were bothered by conflicting green and yellow lights from the jubilant stained glass windows. The minister was a surprisingly young man —"a grand money raiser," who talked fast and through his nose on "Our Lord and Advertising." Everything of value was advertised, and we must not neglect to advertise our Lord and Savior Jesus Christ. Evans sat beside his grandfather, who breathed with difficulty. "Praise God From Whom All Blessings Flow!" they were finally singing. And then Evans was introduced to Brother and Sister,

Brother—Sister, who would say, "What a shame
your mother couldn't come, too! We had hoped to
have her address our missionary society on her work
in the Near East." There seemed great interest in
Mother, because she had been with the missionaries.
Evans thought of Mother's cigarettes, her lip-stick,
and was entertained by this idea of Mother as a
missionary. Yet there was something he liked in
their asking about her as if they knew her.

At dinner he had to talk again, to Aunt Rosie,
about why Mother had been unable to come. "There
are business affairs which keep her in France just
now," he had said at first, and would repeat, firmly.

"I had been counting on it," Aunt Rosie smiled.
"I wanted to see Naomi's little girl." Aunt Rosie
was a plump woman, with red cheeks, and in talking
with you smiled almost all the time, smiling, it
seemed, with her whole face. Yet Evans liked her,
feeling more at home with her than with any of
the others.

"Little girl!" Aunt Agnes laughed. "Guess
Brook's not so many years younger than you, Rosie.
Let's see, how old is your ma, Evans?"

Evans murmured something about not exactly
knowing.

"Well, guess it wouldn't be hard to figure out,"
said Uncle Willie. "Can do it better by myself.
I was seven when Naomi left at nineteen, and Brook
was born that next year. Isn't that so, Caleb?"

"What?" said Grandfather, after a moment of having remained preoccupied with food.

"Yes," said Rosie, "Brook was born that next year."

"Then I was eight when she was born, and guess that makes me eight years older than she is. Being as I'm forty-six, I'd say Brook's thirty-eight. Grace, you're a school-marm, that good arithmetic?"

"I'll mark you one hundred on it, Pa."

But to Evans it did not seem good arithmetic. He looked at Uncle Willie. Only eight years older than Mother? But Uncle Willie was to him an old man, a well-preserved and vigorous old man, differing from Grandfather, a decrepit old man. But Mother—you didn't think of age at all when you looked at Mother.

"Mother and I always wanted to see Naomi's little girl," Aunt Rosie resumed. "Always hoped they'd come home for a visit. This house was never the same place after Naomi left. I remember how it was—those first days. Seems like Mother was always crying—so lonesome for Naomi. And Father, he would sit out there in the kitchen— seemed he was grieving for her. 'I wish we hadn't a let her go,' I heard him say."

"I don't believe there was all that crying and grieving when I left home," laughed Grace.

"Now we missed you, Gracie," her mother assured her. "It was real lonesome when you went."

"Naomi went so far," murmured Naomi's sister Rosie. "And she—there was something about Naomi. . . . Seems to me you favor her," she said to Evans. "Caleb? Caleb! Wouldn't you say Evans favored Naomi?"

Grandfather, more than ever interested in his food—a rather horrid way old people get excited about food—let his fork hover in indecision over the things on his plate. "What say?" he asked. "What say?"

"Wouldn't you say," Aunt Rosie raised her voice, "that Evans favored Naomi?"

His knife and fork, raised, moved back and forth over his plate. "Naomi? Naomi? Seems like I can't remember how she looked!" He was going to cry!

"There—there, Caleb," soothed Aunt Agnes. "You've got your picture of her. Best not," she said low, to Rosie.

"That picture—" He was getting excited, and had not the strength for it. "That was before— *that*—that was when—"

"It's too bad," Aunt Agnes explained, "but there isn't any picture of Naomi except the one here in our album—when she was a girl."

Grandfather had put down his knife and fork. He looked very old—alone—there among them. "Brook would remember. I wish Brook had of come!"

"Mother was so sorry," murmured Evans. "Later," he said—"later," though he knew now that later would be too late.

He had stepped outside with Frank, when Uncle Willie came after them. "Seems like nothing will content Caleb but that you go with him to the cemetery."

"He don't want to do that," Frank objected. "He went to church this morning. That's enough for one day."

But Evans said he didn't mind, that his mother had wanted him to go. Frank would take them, then, in the Chevrolet.

"First I'd like to show Ed and Rosie—well, Evans, too—it's part his—what land 'tis we calculate to sell."

So Aunt Rosie and her husband, one of the children coming along, went with them, walking alongside the brook.

"Seems too bad to sell," said Rosie, "when we always had it."

Buttercups and daisies grew by the brook. He remembered what Mother had come running back to ask. He was going to her mother's grave this afternoon, so he gathered some of the flowers.

"You are fond of flowers?" Aunt Rosie asked. Uncle Ed laughed.

"I am," Evans replied, "but—" somehow he

wanted her to know, "I am gathering these to take to my grandmother's grave."

"Them? they don't amount to nothing," scoffed Uncle Willie. "Your Aunt Agnes'll fix up a cemetery bouquet—roses, things in the flower-beds. You don't have to take *clover*."

"Mother asked me to gather flowers that grew by the brook—" he flushed, but said it, "and take them to her mother's grave."

"Now I think that's a real nice idea!" cried Aunt Rosie. "Seems funny none of us ever thought of it before. Naomi loved the brook."

"Must have set some store by it," agreed her brother, "naming her child for it."

"They were upset at first—Mother and Father," Rosie told Evans, smiling in her way. "Said it didn't seem like a Christian name."

"Well, and so it weren't," Uncle Willie agreed with his parents. "Brook. Brook! Didn't seem like any name at all."

"But now it does," said Rosie. "It's as if Naomi made it a name."

They had followed the brook round a bend; they were out of sight of the house now. The brook curved like an embracing arm, and then above, it again twisted, so that here was a place all by itself, as a little meadow before the sheltering curve of the low hills. An oak reached far over the brook. This place pleased Evans.

" 'Twas a tree grown when I was a boy." Uncle Willie put his hand on the mighty trunk. "One of the oldest round here, I guess."

"Would we sell this, Willie?" Aunt Rosie asked.

"Yes. Begins here, then over the hill, following the brook, 'most as far as the old Copeland place."

"Here's a bluebell, Evans." Aunt Rosie stooped for it, but could not reach across the brook, laughed at her own predicament. "I could have done it once," she sighed. "How we did jump across this brook! Remember, Willie?"

"I remember the wading," said Uncle Willie.

Evans, one foot on a stone in the brook, the other on the far side, stooped for the bluebell, and kept looking into the clear water. These elderly people with him used to play in this stream. And ever since it had gone on, and on—here by itself—so clear. He kept looking into it, as if drawn by something.

"Just climb this rise and I can show you," Uncle Willie proposed.

Evans was last to follow. He let his feet sink into the moss.

"This place has been bought by Germans." Aunt Rosie was chatting with Evans after they had climbed the low hill. "That house is new—well, you could call it new, for there was a big fire there, about fifteen years ago. An old woman—Mrs. Copeland—had shut herself in there for years. She had gone queer, and no one saw her. They had a hard time getting her out the night of the fire. She'd have rather stayed in than face people. She was always kind of queer. Especially after her only son was killed. That was—I was only a little girl."

Evans listened politely.

"Had to take her to the asylum, finally. But she didn't last long there. How much would it be in acres, Willie?"

It seemed Aunt Agnes would never stop talking about the flowers. "But you can have *roses*. The best we've got. Here, 'twill only take a minute."

She was still protesting as he helped his grandfather into Frank's car. "I tell you it just don't seem respectful to me—putting weeds on a grave! And when we've *got* flowers . . ."

CHAPTER XLII

FRANK said he wasn't much of a hand to visit graves—never had been, so while they were "looking round" he'd run on up the road a piece, where he thought he could get the mail. They had teased Frank about his interest in the mail. His girl worked in a store in Davenport.

"If he takes on—just be sharp with him," he advised Evans. "And make him come when you're ready."

But Grandfather did not seem disposed to take on, after they had gone a little way down the hill, followed the path among graves to one which bore the headstone: *"Naomi Kellogg—Beloved Wife of Caleb Evans. Born, 1869. Died, June 12, 1915."* Below, in fancy letters: *"Rest in Peace."*

Grandfather's talk was running along about how he had wanted a different kind of stone, but they didn't have them at the time. "I'll be there," he said, pointing to a place which waited beside this grave of Naomi Kellogg. "They had to chop a tree down to take out roots so's there'd be room for me."

He did not seem depressed by these plans, as he walked over what would be his grave, complaining about the new sexton—seem' like he didn't take as good care of the graves as the old one, but the old one had a grave of his own now.

Several times he thus walked around the grave, then he began to grow excited, whimpering under his breath. "Yes, Naomi—Naomi, she lies buried here. I wouldn't a left her—not out there. She didn't like it. No, never did. She was there—let's see—well, twenty-seven years; and she's been here—let's see—what would you make it, how long now?"

"Twelve years," Evans said. And it came into his mind she would be here longer than she had been there, longer than she had been anywhere.

The flowers had come to seem rather foolish—such a fuss about them, but he kept faith with his mother, carefully placing them near the head of the grave, holding them down by knotting grasses.

"That's for Mother," he explained, not sure his grandfather had understood. "She wanted me to get flowers from the brook."

It seemed to excite his grandfather. "Yes—yes, I know—the brook. The brook. I know! Well, that's all right. That's all right!" His voice was higher. "I—I—" He grasped Evans' arm. "I never told nobody. *Nobody. Not one soul.*"

It was a strange, crafty whisper. Evans had no idea what it meant. Meant nothing, probably.

"So maybe she'll let me lie here by her. Will

you, Naomi?" He was bending over the grave.
He laughed. "Will you, Naomi?" But now he was
beginning to whimper.

Evans took his arm. "I think Frank will be waiting for us."

Across the road his grandfather stopped before a
monument. Evans turned back for a moment alone
by the grave marked Naomi Kellogg. What
there for him to tell his Mother? Graves were
pretty much alike. There was a nice wide look
across the country; though, did it very much matter
what one saw from the top of a grave? Yes, it did.
Somehow, it did. One couldn't say why. He looked
again, now consciously seeing for one who would not
see again. The earth was beautiful, and many who
had known it were now shut from it. When you see
—really see—do you, in a way, see for all who will
not see again?

His grandfather motioned him in from the road.
Evans had had enough of graves now. "Frank will
be waiting," he said, but his grandfather, with uncertainly directed gestures, was pointing to this
monument.

"Copeland."

Where had he heard that name? Oh, this afternoon—the old woman who was queer, and didn't
want to come out of her house, even when it was
burning.

His grandfather was pointing to a name on the

monument, all the while moving from one foot to the other. "How long's *he* been dead? How long's *he* been dead?" There seemed gloating in it—what a dreadful old man, Evans almost let himself think.

"*Joseph Copeland: Born, 1867. Died, July 12, 1888.*"

"He has been dead thirty-nine years," said Evans.

"He has been dead thirty-nine years! And I have been alive all them years. I been alive—all them years he's rotting in the grave!"

"Grandfather!"

But still his grandfather moved from foot to foot, as one dancing a hideous dance of gloating over the dead. He was glad Mother had not come! He would never tell her—how bad it was.

"Reckon the worms have not left much of *him*. Ah—no! Ah—no!" Gloating trailed off into a wail.

Evans was not only outraged, he was interested. That a senile old man could stand dancing up and down before the grave of one long dead, crying out that he himself had been alive while this other was—was . . . It was horrible, but it strangely stirred him.

"What'd he look like *now?*" his grandfather cried. Evans took his arm, saying coldly: "We are going at once."

But as he was leading him away the old man pulled from him, took a backward step, *spat* in the direction of this monument. Not once, but again, and again.

It was with reluctance Evans touched him after this. He was compelled to do so, his grandfather so weak he must have help. "Hope I die young enough to keep decent," the boy thought.

Frank did not see them coming. Across a number of graves Evans saw him in his Chevrolet, smiling as he read the letter from the girl he was going to marry.

At home they had rather a bad time with "the old boy," as Frank called him. The rest of the family had driven over to a neighbor's. Grandfather had a chill, and the three remained in the kitchen, Frank getting him a hot drink. The kitchen was the best room in the house, Evans thought. It was of the old part—a large, sunny room, wide old boards in the floor. "Same kitchen my mother cooked in," Uncle Willie had told him. Grandfather sat by the fire, shuddering.

"Now he's going into one of his spells," Frank said.

"What kind of spells?"

"Melancholy. Won't hear nothing or speak. Mostly stubbornness, that's my opinion."

"Tell you what," he shouted at the old man, "I'm going to see if I can't fix the radio."

This interested Grandfather. "He's the greatest radio fan in the county," Frank laughed. "He's

the real jazz baby. We took it into his room when
he was sick last month, and he got it out of order.
I never seem to have time to fix it. Guess I can,
though."

After Frank had gone, in a stealthy way grandfather began moving to the dining-room.

"What is it?" Evans asked. "I'll get it."

But his grandfather, hand to lips—hunching one
shoulder in crafty, secretive fashion, was moving
through the dining-room into the parlor.

Frank had said the "old boy must sit still for a
while." Should he call Frank? "I'll get anything
you want," Evans said, exasperated.

Again that crafty, silencing gesture, as if he and
Evans were in a conspiracy.

But all he wanted was the album from the parlor
table. His hands shook so he could not lift it.
Evans took it, and in that same stealthy manner the
old man led the way back to the kitchen.

He began excitedly turning the pages, Evans
standing by his chair. Curious old pictures. Strange
clothes they used to wear. Men—women—children; life had been going on for them when these
pictures were taken. They were in the midst of
things then. Now they had been—out of it, a long
time. Had they been—quite different from us?
They looked different. Yet you saw familiar things:
kindness—sometimes amusement. Usually they
looked as if they felt foolish—dressed up having

their pictures taken. Some looked severe. Some tired.

Grandfather was having trouble finding the picture he wanted, but at last: "A—h," and in an excited, secretive way, he motioned Evans to bend closer.

It was a girl. How quaint that ruffled dress! Her hair was done low. Slim—stooping just a little, like a flower. Something about her—one knew one would like her. It was the eyes—the mouth—as if she saw, felt things.

"Naomi—" his grandfather murmured. "Naomi."

So this was his grandmother! But she—how could she ever have married *this* man? For she was, one saw it, a quite different sort of person—different from any of them here. Sunlight strayed across the picture. It was brown—old; but something in those eyes as they looked up at Evans—time had not hurt that look. It was here for Evans—the gentle look of one who saw, felt things. So *she* was here, too, behind him—not just these others. He was glad. Strange that Mother had talked of her father, and so little of her mother.

A crash of jazz, *"There ain't no maybe in my baby's eyes!"*

"Chicago!" his grandfather cried, and would have dropped the album if Evans had not taken it.

Evans sat alone in the sunny kitchen, looking at the picture of the young girl—Naomi—his grandmother. Sunlight and shadow moved over the picture. He wished the light could move back into the years. He would like to know—how it had been with her. He could not know. The years were dark shadow in between. But something in her eyes—about her mouth . . . Thinking of her he looked from the window, through trees to the brook. He could not hear the brook now, because of the radio.

"Well, now he's happy," Frank laughed. "A jazz revival hour. All the old favorites. He wants you to come in and listen."

Evans wanted his tramp now, but after he had returned the album he looked into his grandfather's room.

The emaciated old man sat before an enormous horn, his hands, head, moving grotesquely with the music. *"Though you belong to somebody else—tonight you belong to me!"*

"Chicago!" he cried. "The roof!" He wagged his head. "Good reception! Good reception!"

"My baby knows how!" screamed Chicago into this old room.

A nice room—low ceiling; here too the wide old boards. Standing just right you could see the brook. The garage shouldn't have been put there.

"Hallelujah!" Great for dancing, this one. *"Sing Hallelujah—Hallelujah!"* Would he get any dancing in America? When he went back East he would go to Washington, an American officer, old

friend of his father. Then the Ellsworths in New York—people Mother had known in Constantinople, later in Paris. And the Blakemans—nice family he met on the ship, pretty girl—jolly, not silly. *"Hallelujah—Hallelujah!—"* Evans was dancing, the kind of dancing like talking under one's breath, then stopped, seeing his grandfather, too, did this, and it was too weird—an old man about to fall into his grave—why should he be jerking and wagging like this?

"Me and My Shadow!"

This could be a nice room. Too bad they had put in the white iron bed. These honest old boards wanted to support a four-poster, something of weight. Several pieces of the heavy old walnut furniture remained. The bureau must have been in just this place for years, for the boards before it were worn down, as by one who stood there. This window-sill, too, curved a little, smoothed by hands that had rested there, as some one looked out at the brook, perhaps. Must have seen the brook from this window before the garage went up.

"Why am I so lonely? Will I die so lonely?" asked Chicago, with violence. It was as if the horn were attacking. The sound-waves came too strong, and the old walls sent them back, not wanting them, not willing to let them sink into the room.

Evans yawned. Bored. Stuffy. Get out now for a tramp.

"Sorry!" squealed the radio.

Come to think of it, many of the songs were about being lonely, or being sorry, or wanting to be somewhere else.

Aunt Agnes was returning. "Well—say!" Frank came in. "Kick me—will you?" He held out a letter. "So interested in my own," he grinned, "I forgot yours."

His grandfather continued to sit immediately in front of the horn that belched music:

> *"First love is the best love!*
> *There's a rapture,*
> *You can't recapture."*

"Right-oh," said Frank, tapping him on the back. "Atta boy! Atta boy!"—looked up to wink at Evans, before he went dancing out.

The letter was from Mother; Aunt Agnes had gone upstairs. Better get right away—out this back door, around the barn, then into the trees and up the brook. If she knew he were going she would insist some one go with him—"for company." Grandfather was now stupefied by jazz; Evans left him before the wide-mouthed horn, his head and hands moving as if he were a decrepit automaton, while a Chicago cabaret told him to mix Cleopatra and Camille—add a dash of sex appeal—and what do you get? *Mag*nolia!

Evans followed the stream until he came to that

place he had liked, where the brook became as a curving arm, granting a secluded place before the low hills. He lay under the oak, his hand on the deep moss. Mother's letter. But for the moment he lay listening to the brook—to the sound in the great trees. This was as a secret place. Did no one ever come here?

CHAPTER XLIII

"DARLING BOY," his mother wrote. "I have something to tell you. It will explain why I did not go with you to America. Only, will it explain? Will you understand?

"My son, forgive me for the abruptness with which I must tell you what should not come to you like this.

"Dear, I am married. Now! You know now. Oh, you will forgive me—won't you, dear? Let me tell you.

"You saw him a little while one evening. I think he interested you. Erik Helge—from Iceland. The Colonel did not like him, but I think you did. You would, I am sure—will, when you know him."

Evans could not read on. He could not believe what it was he saw. Why—he didn't even know Mother knew this man! He hadn't known there *was* such a man! She had never spoken of him. Where had she known him? Not at the house. He had been there—that Evans knew of—only once.

Mother! *Married.* And to a stranger—this strange person. Evans tried to remember how he looked—what he had said. He had been interested in him, that was true, but not—he didn't seem the kind of a person to marry! For Mother to marry! No, the Colonel didn't approve of him—didn't know him. Who did know him? Who was he? He read on:

"I did not tell you before because I myself didn't know it—until just at the last. I confess I have known Erik only a very little while.

"This will startle—seem undignified to you. It does not seem that to me, because to me it seems inevitable. I love him. I am happy."

Evans' hand shut upon the letter. She loved him. She was happy. Then Father— He seemed to meet his father's eyes, as that last time, when he said, "Take your mother for a drive." That look—afterwards he knew it for a brave look—and when he came home . . . The boy lay flat on the earth, face pressed into the moss, trying—trying to bear it—not to curse—not to cry—to keep still a moment, keep *still*. One arm was around his head, the other pounded the ground with his fist.

Father? *This* was what it was for then—that courage, courage to put himself out of it—releasing Mother. And for—for this *stranger*. *"I love him. I am happy."* And Father was in one of those graves—forgotten.

The sobs would not hold back. He burrowed his face into the soft moss. Horrible things that old man had said— "What'd he look like *now*—" "Oh, Jesus!" the boy cried. "God damn it!"

He started running up the brook—went a long way before he slowed to a walk.

So Mother had kicked it all over—Father, him, her own father, the Colonel—given up the whole past—gone off by herself—this stranger.

"Take your mother for a drive." She had cried because her hair was turning gray. But it didn't turn gray, Evans thought bitterly. She needn't have cried over it. How wonderfully Father had done it —there by himself—so little time, managing it so there would be nothing of suspicion, no reproach, the least of pain. That letter to his own mother, in London then: "Ask Doctor Forbes to come down and see me. I don't want to alarm you, Forbes can fix me up—but just in the last half-hour—a pain— round the heart—different kind of pain—tell Forbes—"

That unfinished letter lay on his bed.

So no one had suspected—and why had *he*—why had Evans? He didn't really—or didn't let himself know he did. Father had been in pain. Had he been able to get one of the tablets? Evans had given him one two nights before. There had been eight—seven left in the box. Now there was one left in the box.

So he took away all the medicine, and when his

grandmother spoke of it, saying, "We mustn't leave it around,"—"I disposed of it all," he said. "I didn't like to see it." "Yes," she murmured, crying, "yes, dear."

The rotten time Father had had! For years. *"I love him. I am happy."*

And Mother had sent him out here to square it with her relatives. Vulgar, stupid people—*common.* He wished he had never seen them—didn't have to know he was related to them. That old man— *what* a grandfather—nauseating—spitting at graves —then listening in at "Red Hot Baby!" He'd leave to-morrow! He didn't have to stay here. He'd go back to his Grandmother Leonard. He'd live in England—be like his father—the kind of person who didn't throw everybody down for—for— Or else he'd go to the devil. Why not? Who was there to stop him? Who had the right to say anything to him now? Well, who wanted to? Who cared?

Anger that made him kick things out of the way. Tears that blinded.

He had given no heed where he went. Now he found himself on the highway, too many cars passing. Should he turn back? Why should he? How could he sit there with them at supper-time—knowing this? One of these cars would give him a lift— somewhere.

He felt in his pockets. Oh, why be a fool, he

thought, suddenly weary. He had to have his
clothes—money. And the fuss they would make!
He could almost smile as he thought of the fuss
Aunt Agnes would make.

He walked back slowly—tired, feeling that he
walked alone, that he was indeed alone now.

He heard the brook before he came to it. He was
glad to hear it, and went down the little hill to join
it; walking slowly—himself not thinking, but letting
the brook keep him company. A robin flew from his
bath. "Never mind," Evans assured. "Needn't
go." Well, he could talk to a bird again, anyway.
The brook was so clear. It made this music—here
all by itself.

Then the brook turned, and when he came upon
that place he liked—it was as if he came back to a
secret place he had known a long time. He lay on
the moss by the oak-tree, closed his eyes, and the
brook was like a friend. It was as if he didn't have
to go on pounding it out by himself—wanting to
fight, crying; no, the brook was something more than
any of that. "Intimations." What was it about
intimations? Oh, yes—name of that volume of
poems—the day Mother bought the dress—acting
so strangely about it. For *him,* probably. Yes, that
was it—though she said her mother. Nonsense
that—a lot of bologny, Frank would say—her
mother had been dead for years. Well—never
mind, never mind all that now—no use trying to

dope it out. Intimations. From where? Intimations—of what?

Quiet now—quieted by the brook, as if it had healing. He smoothed out his mother's letter.

"We are going to China." *China.* Evans laughed. Why, the thing was crazy! Then something about work—mathematics, original, brilliant—had genius.

"My dear, dear son—we have gone through long hard things together. They have made you older than your years. So I think—though perhaps not at first—you may understand. There are these years left for me—not too many. I want them. I confess —I want them. I would fight for them. But not you, dear—surely that need not be. I think Father would want me to be happy."

He put his hand over his eyes, shaking his head as if to shake something away. Father was in one of those graves now.

Or—was he? Thinking went from him, as pain can go from one, mercifully releasing. Leaning against the tree that was there for him, he heard the brook, scarcely knowing he heard it—intimations— intimations that did not come into words.

Father in his grave? But he seemed to hear his voice. "Well, old man, if I can stand it, can't you? Better buck up now. *Who* had a long hard time? Your mother had a long hard time." Once more he met his father's eyes, so brave they did not let you know they were brave. Graves? Oh, yes. But that which could live!

Again he took up his mother's letter. About him now. Would he care to stay on and go to school in America? Mr. Ellsworth, in New York, would arrange it. "They say America is the country of the future. And it's your country—if you want it to be. You are from America as well as from England. Your own money, dear. Of course that has never been touched. There is enough. Or do you wish to go to England—until I know a little more of how things are with me, and then perhaps you would like to come to China. Why not? An adventure. Life is adventure, dear. That's why I couldn't marry the Colonel."

The Colonel. That would have seemed—going on with something for Father. Going on with their old life. That would not have left Father behind. This left him—so far behind. "Well, old man, if I can stand it . . ." Strange how things his father had never said to him were said now, said from— from intimations? Were they—the intimations— out of that place from which we do not speak? Were they from what we know, and never say we know, or only half know—dimly—and was it from there we sometimes—almost reached one another?

There seemed something that did not die.

Adventure. Life was adventure. In the past, too, adventure. Father had had to stop. He had not wanted Mother to stop. Father had one—great adventure. Greater than the war. Greater than anything in life. He had had the courage not to say one farewell word. Not to flick an eyelash. Was that to come to nothing? Mother didn't know. But he—Evans—knew. This was something between him and his father. Father had guarded her. Then he must guard her now. All right. All right, then. Sure. He would stand by Mother.

Something lost—something won—he lay back and let his head rest on the deep moss. Through the oak-branches he saw the first star. He smelled drying grass—the new hay. The brook and the trees—this pure clear sound of the brook within the more freely moving sound of the trees—music—intimations. Graves, yes; but those eyes that looked up at him from the old album—Naomi—his grandmother. What did they say? He did not know. He did not exactly know. Yes, he would stand by his mother. Love. He didn't know it yet. Some day. Yes, perhaps. He felt close to all who were in their graves. He closed his eyes and listened. The wind passed over his face. Through all the future it would flow softly—with deep sweet meaning—with mystery—this hour—intimations from the brook.

THE END